PEPPERMINT WISHES

D.L. DARBY

peppermint wishes

d.l. darby

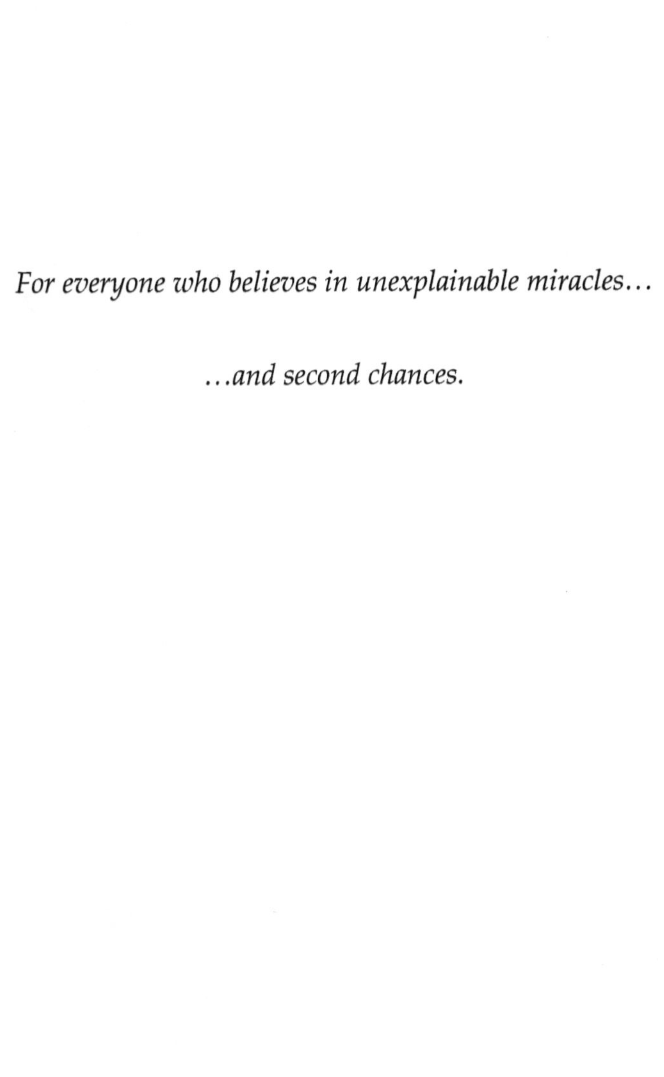

For everyone who believes in unexplainable miracles…

…and second chances.

content warning

This book contains talk of spousal cheating, miscarriage, and off-page death.

Please read responsibly.

a note from the author

This is not a romance. This is a love story.

Yes, it has a HEA. It just may not be the type you're thinking.

I'll always feel you close to me and though you're far from sight, I'll search for you among the stars that shine on Christmas night.

— Unknown

prologue

They say if you love something, set it free. If it comes back, it's yours. If not, it was never meant to be.

To say my soon-to-be ex-husband did *not* love me would be a gross understatement. Steven Parker Montgomery loves himself, the house we bought six years ago and remodeled together, and his newly pregnant girlfriend–soon-to-be wife–once our divorce is finalized.

She already has kids of her own and plans to move them into the rooms where I painted murals of baby woodland creatures and wildflowers. A nursery and a playroom that I never had the chance to fill with shrill baby cries and loud toddler laughter.

My bags were barely packed before she'd come in and started explaining to Steven everything she wanted to change about the place. Stars had shone in his eyes as he looked at her, belly round and full of his progeny.

If only my body would have cooperated, then perhaps he wouldn't have strayed. Wouldn't have gone seeking companionship from the secretary who was all too happy to step in and take the place of the wife who couldn't give him what he truly desired in life.

A family.

The anger has long since faded. Sure, it sucks. I'd be lying if I said I wasn't still a little sad about it. But, honestly, why mourn the loss of someone who doesn't want you anymore? Steven is a dick, and I'm young. Thirty-two and healthy–aside from my lack of ability to grow a child.

I want to travel and see the world and all it has to offer. To feel sand between my toes while the sun shines on my face and water laps at my ankles. Sip piña coladas while a tanned, muscular man shows me how to salsa. Hike Mt. Kilimanjaro. Go on safari. Snorkel in the Caribbean.

My life is going to be a damn good one. That, I'm sure of.

I just have to get through Christmas.

It is, poetically, my favorite and least favorite time of the year. I've always loved the bright lights, the peppermint candy canes, and the hot chocolate while caroling around my parents' neighborhood. The smell of pine and cinnamon, freshly baked gingerbread, and the whiskey my father always poured in his eggnog.

Those are the good memories. The ones I never want to let go of. But then there is the yearly reminder that, two years ago, my parents died on Christmas. They were traveling from their home in Sutton, Wyoming, to visit me in Denver. A snowstorm had raged wind and ice so harshly that day, and I'd told them to wait it out. However, Steven was away on a work trip, and my parents had always insisted that *"no one should be alone on Christmas."*

A semi-truck lost control and hit them head-on. My only comfort was that they died instantly, according to the paramedics on the scene. The accident took five lives that Christmas.

After Steven announced his affair, I'd decided to move back to Sutton. To take the time I was supposed to be grieving my marriage to clean out my parents' house and finally put it on the market.

It was time to let go. Time for a fresh start.

However, memories of past holidays were too hard to deal with alone in their house. So, I booked a cabin up at Sutton Lake, around thirty minutes outside of town, to spend the Christmas weekend at.

I've adopted my parents' sentiment that no one should be alone on Christmas. But since it was inevitable, I might as well be isolated and far enough away from civilization, that no one will hear my drunken cries as I drown the pain from missing them in a bottle of vodka.

chapter one

"*S*hit!"

The taste of blood mixes with the sweet mint of the candy cane I'm sucking on as the sharp point I've formed pierces my tongue. A crunch fills my ears as I bite the end off and chew as if punishing the candy for the crime I forced it to commit.

Fat, heavy flakes fall slowly outside as I drive toward my destination, Sutton Lake. *A cozy cabin nestled on the bank of the lake. Fully decked out for Christmas! Stockings are hung by the chimney with care! With a tree for St. Nick to put presents under there!* the Vrbo listing had read.

All I want St. Nick to bring me is a cash offer on my parents' house, and a one-way ticket to Europe.

Nat King Cole croons "The Christmas Song" on

the radio as I finish my candy cane and reach for another from the pile in the passenger seat. Any other month of the year, I wanted nothing to do with the red and white striped sugar sticks. But from the middle of December till the beginning of January, they might as well be their own food group in my extremely unbalanced diet.

After I unwrap the end of the cane and put it in my mouth, I run my hand through my long, bright blonde hair. Frowning around the candy as the stickiness of my fingers gets caught in the freshly washed strands, I roll my fingers together to release the hair I pulled out.

"This is what I get for attempting to look like something other than a trash panda."

If it were summer, I'd let my knee take the wheel as I attempt to wrestle my mane into a haphazard messy bun. However, since the roads are icy and my attention needs to be focused solely on driving safely, the trash panda in me will have to wait just a little while longer until I get to the cabin.

Ten more minutes of old Christmas songs and consecutive candy cane eating, and I'd arrive at my destination according to the GPS. The snow-capped mountains glitter in the afternoon sunlight, and the frosted ponderosas cage the road as if trying to hug my car.

"Welcome to our beautiful home." They seem to say.

It *is* beautiful up here. Absolutely breathtaking. And I wonder why we never camped in this area when I was a kid. My dad used to love taking us on camping trips. It seemed odd that he'd overlooked such a beautiful location so close to home. Then again, it seems pretty isolated, and my parents had liked making friends on our trips.

My eyes don't stray from the road for long as I take in the surroundings. The sky is dimming, filled with the promise of more snow through the evening. The road finally curves off to the right, but I steer my Chevy Malibu left, following the GPS instructions and turning onto what I assume is a dirt road when the harsh winter lifts its cold spell on this part of the world.

Five more minutes of nothing but twists and turns, and I finally pull into the driveway for the cabin. From its listing, I expect a small log cabin–there are no exterior photos–but what stares back at me is a beautiful, roomy, two-story A-frame made of cedar with a black asphalt shingle roof. There's a lower deck that wraps around the entire cabin, and a balcony off what I assume is the master bedroom, that overlooks the lake.

No trees obstruct the view of the frozen water that's covered in a layer of mostly undisturbed snow.

Drifts have been formed in numerous places on the lake's surface, making them look like thick dollops of glittery frosting. On the other side of the lake is another cabin, huge and equally as beautiful as this one. Smoke curls up from the chimney–a sign that someone is there–and a black truck is parked outside.

Briefly, I worry that the noise of my predestined Christmas meltdown will carry across the lake and disturb my neighbors.

As I step out of my car, the air shifts to the East–toward the lake. The flakes that have been falling the entire drive up have ceased, and the shoveled path leading from the driveway to the stairs is still fresh enough that my bright pink, hard-shell suitcase rolls easily behind me. There are only a few stairs that shepherd me to the front door and a four-digit code that separates the outside world from the warmth inside the cabin.

My eyes widen as I look around before stepping over the threshold and shutting the door behind me, abandoning my suitcase at the front door. It looks like Christmas threw up in here. Garland is wrapped around the rafters and railings leading to the second story. A large tree stands in the corner, fully decorated with a bright, glowing star at the top. Stockings have indeed been hung by the chimney, the skinny old brick fireplace still glowing with the embers of a previous fire.

The hosts must not have left that long ago if they trusted leaving the cabin unattended with a fire going.

Walking further inside to place my purse and keys on the large kitchen counter, the scent of apples and cinnamon invades my senses. A red, square dish sits on the counter covered in plastic wrap with toothpicks holding it up, and a small note beside the dish reads:

Happy Holidays!

We hope you enjoy your stay!

Tossing the note aside, I peel the plastic off the dish to find glazed apple cinnamon rolls. Carbs? Fucking yes, please! Pulling one out, I take a bite and moan in ecstasy as the light icing glaze melts on my tongue.

Silver garland hangs from the front of the counter, and greenery dotted with red berries and poinsettias drapes over the top of the light-washed cabinets. What isn't Christmas-themed is decorated in red and black flannel with touches of green and blue here and there. A brown leather sofa sits in front of the fire-place with a fuzzy red and black checkered throw over the back of it. Curtains that look like they are more for decoration than keeping the sun out are gathered on either side of the large windows. Clear sparkling Christmas lights are entwined with the green garland on the rafters, creating a buttery glow throughout the whole place.

"Mom, Dad, you guys would have loved it here," I whisper to myself as I make my way to the second story.

The decorations aren't as plentiful up here. A simple, queen-sized bed sits against the wall, centered across from the double doors that lead out onto the balcony I saw outside. It's covered in a thick red quilt with navy sheets and pillows. A small wood stove sits in the corner on a stone hearth, a pile of firewood stacked behind it.

With a sigh, I flop onto the bed, careful not to fling the snow from my Adirondack boots every-where. I should have taken them off when I came inside. Shoving the rest of the cinnamon roll in my mouth, I chew slowly while unbuttoning my black and white flannel shacket. My suitcase is full of fleece-lined leggings, thick Merino wool socks, and oversized comfy turtleneck sweaters. And since heat rises, I have a feeling I'll be sweating all night if I sleep in the bed.

Something flashes in my peripheral, and I turn my head to see that the heavy snowflakes from earlier are falling again. Heavier, fatter, and faster. Their rhythmic freefall creates a hypnotic sensation as I feel my eyes start to droop. In the back of my mind, I know it's too late for a nap, but it's not like I have any plans later.

So, I let the snowflakes, the warmth of the cabin, and the homey scent of apple cinnamon lull me to sleep like they're my personal, perceptional, winter wonderland lullaby.

chapter two

Silence greets me when I awaken. Not the normal kind, but a heavy, thick quiet that makes you think someone has entered the room. The snow is still falling outside. Whatever light that's left from the sun has been swallowed by weighty gray clouds.

My head feels heavy, partly from sleep and partly from shoving the cinnamon roll down my throat before passing out. Gluten has never been my friend, but we only have one life to live, and I'll be damned if I wasn't going to eat whatever I wanted until the end of my days.

As I descend the stairs, I notice the embers in the fireplace have gone out completely. There is no firewood for this one like there is upstairs, but through the window, I can see a tiny woodshed off to the side of the cabin. A small path looks like it had been shoveled, but it's now covered in fresh powder.

It's still decidedly warm inside, so I forgo going back upstairs to retrieve my jacket, my feet still nestled in my boots from earlier since I forgot to take them off before my nap. As I make my way outside and down the path to get more wood, I notice there's a bright orange sled tied to the shed, assumingly for hauling said wood. I count that as a win because the sharp, biting cold has already eaten its way through my leggings and cream knit sweater.

Hurriedly, I untie the sled and turn to start grabbing wood from a pile that stands taller than two of me put together. The wind picks up while I play real-life Jenga, and a forceful gust sends me stumbling back. One boot kicks the sled while the other steps in it, causing me to fall ass-first into the sled, the wood in my arms weighing me down.

Suddenly, the wind is more fierce, and my heart drops into my stomach as the sled starts moving backward. "AHHH!"

Flurries kick up all around me as it picks up speed, careening down the small hill that leads to the lake. The cabin gets further and further away as I scramble to try to regain my balance and stop this unwarranted sleigh ride.

When I was a kid, and my parents would take me sledding, my mom would always roll us out if the sled got too unruly. But as I prepare myself to steamroll and escape, I let out an abrupt scream as I'm hurled into the air from the sled launching off a snowdrift like an Olympic ski jumper.

The breath is knocked from my lungs as the sled lands roughly, and I'm flung back. Even though I can't see where I'm going, I know I'm now on the lake as the wind whips snow all around me, continuing to push the sled with an unusual Herculean force. Every time I try to grip the sides and push myself out, another gust of violent wind whips me back down. Tears line my eyes from the cold, as chips of ice and snow tear at my face.

Distantly, I hear someone shouting, and suddenly the wind dies down as the sled starts to slow. The sound of footsteps crunching over the snow grows closer as I lay there, wiping my ratted hair out of my face and wondering how the hell I was going to trudge back to the cabin with no jacket. As if to drive that point home, I start to shiver as the snow begins to melt on my skin.

"Are you okay? That was quite the show," a deep, gritty tenor cuts through my thoughts.

"No, I'm not okay! What kind of question is that?! The wind just served me a literal *fuck you*," I wail, as I jackknife into a sitting position and wrap my arms around myself before turning around.

To see the most beautiful steel blue eyes staring down at me.

My teeth begin to chatter, sounding like a woodpecker hammering away at a tree, as I continue to stare up at the man. He's tall, but then again, I'm still sitting on my ass in the sled, surrounded by snow and the few pieces of firewood that managed to stick with me for the windy ride. Anyone would seem tall in my position.

He offers me a hand, and I take it, wobbling as I attempt to stand while the sled tries to glide out from underneath me. Both his hands wrap around my arms in an attempt to steady me as I nearly fall into him.

"Sorry for yelling. That was just the most bizarre thing that's ever happened to me," I manage in between the continuous noise of my teeth.

He shrugs out of his thick, black Carhartt jacket before placing it around my shoulders. "I don't think I've ever seen anything quite like whatever that just was. It hasn't been that windy up here lately, and that gust carried you clear across the lake."

Turning, I see that my cabin is indeed quite far away, and my shoulders sag at the thought of having to walk back to it in the cold.

"Name's Jonathan. And you are?" He reaches out a hand for me to shake as he introduces himself. He *is* tall.

Tall and handsome, with a head full of dark hair and a smile that nearly blinds me, glowing as bright as the star on the tree in my cabin. He's also got an untrimmed beard that looks like it's three weeks old. I love beards.

"Cold. Extremely cold. And you're going to freeze if I keep your jacket. What are you doing out here anyway?" I lean around him to see that he's got a fishing pole and an ice auger lying on the ground, not that far away. The wind really *did* kick my ass clear across the lake.

He laughs and sticks his hands in his pockets as he hunches his shoulders. The cold is clearly setting in already, despite his thick flannel button-up and what looks like a plain black sweater underneath.

"The walleye are more active at night," he explains. "Was planning on catching a few before your screeching alerted me to your little spectacle. Probably scared all the fish away, too."

Screeching?!

"You act like I did all that on purpose! Trust me, walking back across the lake without proper clothes was the last thing on my mind. I just wanted some firewood to get me through the night."

"Well, considering my cabin is closer than yours, why don't you let me drive you back over there?"

My ears perk up at his exclamation, and I realize that Jonathan must own the cabin across the lake from mine. So much for trying not to disturb my neighbors. Consider my Christmas meltdown in full swing already.

He's shivering as he looks at me expectantly, growing visibly more annoyed the longer I take to answer him. "Look, if you want to walk back on your own, that's fine by me. Call the jacket a favor for now, and you can bring it over to me later."

Turning, he starts to mutter something about doing nice things for people and stuck-up princess Barbies.

He thinks I look like Barbie?

"Wait!" I shout at his retreating back. "I'm sorry. It's been a day. Well, it's been a weird couple of months, actually. Christmas is a hard time for me. I didn't mean to be so rude. I'm Evelyn."

Rambling, I hurry to catch up to him because he doesn't stop in his rush to get back to his cabin. He leaves the pole and the ice auger, and I wonder if I should grab them before realizing there's no way I could drag the auger without having to take my hands out of the sleeves of his jacket.

The night is progressing quickly, and the air is becoming chillier, nipping at every part of me like the sting of a rubber band being snapped against your skin. My fingers are nearly numb, and Jonathan looks like he's freezing now that I'm cocooned in his jacket.

He's still mumbling to himself, but at this point, I can't make out anything he's saying. We reach the edge of the lake and ascend the small hill that leads up to his cabin. I'm thankful the path is shoveled and has a layer of sand to prevent slipping.

Jonathan's cabin is beautiful. It's all bright pine and stone, with a matching wrap-around deck. There are large windows scattered across the front, allowing a glimpse into the golden glow of the interior. The only thing missing is Christmas decorations. Maybe I'm dealing with a real-life Scrooge.

"This is beautiful. Is it yours?"

His response comes out gruff and gritty. "Yes."

Well, it seems I've thoroughly pissed off my neighbor.

As we reach the entrance, I'm still looking at my surroundings when I run into his back. He's frozen, with the door open slightly and one foot over the threshold. His head turns to the side as he addresses me. "I'll just be a moment. The truck is unlocked, and the keys are in it if you want to warm up."

With that, he slips inside and shuts the door in my face.

chapter three

Silence has never been my strong suit.

Ever since I was a kid, my parents would always laugh when my teachers would tell them, "She talks a lot. Like, a lot. Very sociable. Has a comment for everything. It can be very disruptive. She really needs to work on knowing when to focus and pay attention."

In the last few months, I've been quiet. Most of my friends were also Steven's, and when news broke of our divorce–even though it was due to *him* cheating–they picked him. The only person I have to talk to is my cousin, Kendall. But she lives in Chicago and is a busy woman, so she picks up when she can, but it isn't often.

Chalk it up to the fact that I've spent months talking out loud to my dead parents–or that I have no candy canes to stick in my mouth–that no matter how hard I try, I can't keep silent on the drive.

"I don't think this is the way back to my cabin." My gaze focuses out the window on the trees. The wind playing a game of cat and mouse with the snow on their branches, kicking up flurries against the indigo sky.

"I need to stop in town. Figured we'd do that first." Jonathan's tone is quiet and contemplative. He's shifted his weight onto his left side, angling himself away from me. When I take the time to assess his body language, he actually looks quite uncomfortable.

Shrugging, I lean back in my seat and cross my arms over my chest. His oversized jacket swallows my frame as I snuggle deeper into it, the scent of balsam fir and woodchips engulfing my senses. "I didn't realize there was a town close to here. It's weird. I grew up in Sutton and never even knew about the cabins at the lake. What town are we going to?"

"Lake Town."

"Ahh. They must have rebuilt after the whole Smaug thing."

He looks over at me and raises an eyebrow. I shoot him an incredulous look and exclaim, "The Hobbit? Lake-town? Tolkien?"

Jonathan shakes his head slowly, like he has no clue what I'm talking about.

"You've never heard of The Hobbit?!"

"Why are you screeching?" he drawls. "Yes, I've heard of The Hobbit. Just never read it or watched the movies."

My mouth drops open at his admission. He glances over at me and tries not to laugh, but fails miserably. "I don't watch a lot of TV."

"If we were friends, I would tell you what an absolute travesty it is that you haven't seen those movies. Lord of the Rings?"

"Nope."

"Well, that's a damn shame."

The trees begin to thin out as businesses start coming into view. Colorful buildings, all decked out for Christmas, line the streets. It's the type of town where people wave as you drive past–though Jonathan doesn't wave back at any of them. I return a wave or two and offer a friendly smile as we roll slowly through the main street.

"I need to grab some groceries. There's a coffee shop on the other side of the street if you want to wait there, or you can wait in the truck." He pulls into a small parking lot with barely room for twenty or so cars.

"What? Are you afraid to be seen with me? Am I

not allowed in the grocery store?" It's a joke, but I don't miss the way he slightly tenses as I say it.

With a slight shrug, he replies, "I don't care if you come in or not."

He puts the truck in park and doesn't wait for me to say whether or not I'm going to stay. Turning it off, he opens the door and makes his way toward the small store. Not wanting to be left behind as the truck grows cold, I clamor out of my side and catch up as he lifts his keys over his shoulder and presses lock on the key fob.

Jonathan grabs a cart once we're inside as I look around the small area. It's tinier than a Walgreens, more of a small mom-and-pop store. As we pass the checkout area, I notice a bowl filled with small individually wrapped candy canes and grab one, immediately relaxing as the cool peppermint hits my tongue.

"You gonna pay for that?" Jonathan asks.

Does this guy have eyes in the back of his head or something?

"I have cash at my house. I thought they were free." My cheeks redden. Lowering my head, I glance around to see if anyone else saw me.

We pass rows of home goods, plastic products for the kitchen, and an aisle for pets, until finally, we reach his destination. The meat and produce department.

He's quick to greet the burly butcher behind the meat counter, who stares at me curiously as though he's not sure I'm a real person and he's wondering if Jonathan can see me. I suppose I do look like a mess, with my windblown hair, swimming in Jonathan's jacket.

"Want your usual?" the butcher asks him.

"Yeah, make it a twelve-ounce today, please, Tommy."

"Just the one steak?" Tommy's uptalk is prying, and I shove my chin into my shoulder, attempting to hide my grin. His eyes ping-pong between Jonathan and me, and I swear he slightly jerks his head in my direction.

"Just the one, Tommy." Jonathan turns to me and jerks his head to the counter. "Did you need to grab anything?"

"No. I'm fine with the cinnamon rolls the hosts made. Plus, I brought snacks."

"Snacks? For the whole weekend?"

"I'm not fond of cooking, if I'm being honest. So, yeah. Snacks."

"You know, if it's a money thing, you can pay me back when we get to your cabin."

My shoes become the most interesting thing in the store as I tell him, "It has nothing to do with that! I just told you I don't cook."

Steven did the cooking. I can barely boil water

without it bubbling over and burning my hand in the process.

He makes a humming noise before asking, "So, what were you planning on eating for Christmas dinner?" He sounds like he's scolding a child, and I have the distinct urge to say, *"Knock it off, Dad."*

Instead, I shrug and parry with, "I'm going to be alone. What does it matter if I eat a cooked meal?"

"I didn't realize you would be alone. I just assumed you'd have someone coming to meet you." A look of concern, or perhaps just sympathy, crosses his face as I look back up. Strangely, I find myself wanting him to know that it's *just* me alone in the cabin across the lake from his.

"No, it's just me." Pausing, I tear my gaze away and focus on the juicy ribeye cuts that are in front of us in the glass case. Tommy's back is to us as he packages up Jonathan's steak, and I'm grateful I've lost half my audience as I say, "I'm going through a divorce. He left me for his secretary."

I don't know why I tell him the second part. I could have stopped at divorce, and it would have been just fine.

"Fucking cliche," Jonathan sighs as he shakes his head.

Don't I know it.

"Eh, I know. But I like to think I came out on top.

Now I get to eat, pray, love my way through all the other continents."

"*All* the continents?"

"Oh yeah. I hear Antarctica has lots of prospects."

He doesn't laugh at my joke, and embarrassment starts to settle in as the silence stretches between us.

My mouth is void of its comfort candy, and I think about going back to the front to grab a handful of peppermint sticks from the bowl as a way to escape the palpable pity radiating off him. Jonathan's voice cuts through my thoughts, though, and glues my feet to the floor.

"He's a fucking idiot."

Tommy hands him his steak over the counter and gives me a nod before turning his back to us again. As Jonathan walks away, I can't help the smile that forms on my face. "What about you?"

"What about me?"

"I notice you only got one steak. No one's joining *you* this weekend?"

It's evident that I've hit a nerve by the way his hands tighten on the shopping cart as he stops, and the way he lets out a shuddered exhale. I don't mean to pry, but I want to know more about this man.

"I'm sorry, you don't have to answer that." Shaking my head, I walk away. I have no idea where I'm going, but it's clear that I made him uncomfortable, and I know firsthand that's not a fun pit to be thrown into.

"It's...fine. It's just me," he answers tightly, moving the cart forward again.

We're silent as he picks out a few heads of broccoli and studies the state of the ripe red strawberries before putting two containers in the cart. He also grabs a package of romaine lettuce, a few carrots, and some radishes—-at which I grimace and inwardly gag.

Since the night is growing late, I decide to come back into town tomorrow to look around myself and pick up a few things to get me through the long weekend. After all, my stomach probably won't be too happy if all I feed it is cinnamon rolls, packages of Pop-Tarts, and beef jerky.

My stomach grumbles as I think about food–just as Jonathan passes by. He stops and raises an eyebrow at me, and my cheeks flush crimson in embarrassment. He reaches into the pocket of his red and black flannel jacket and pulls out one of the miniature candy canes from the bowl at the front of the store, and holds it out to me like we're doing a drug deal.

As I take it, he grabs another from his pocket, and I laugh lightly as I tear into mine. "Okay, peppermint ninja. I'm going to assume these were already in there because I didn't see you grab any."

He grins down at me, and it catches me off guard.

Jonathan's smile is like staring into the sun. It lights up his whole face. His eyes sparkle, and his teeth gleam. And I have to tear my eyes away from his because now my cheeks are flushed for an entirely different reason. As are other parts of my body that haven't been in use for quite a while. Pretty sure there are cobwebs in places one should never have cobwebs.

"Don't tell anyone," he whispers.

My hands reach up, pretending I'm locking my lips before acting like I'm tossing a key over my shoulder. With the other hand, I stick the candy in my mouth, my fingers looped around the hooked end, as I let my attention fall back to the food around us.

Jonathan picks up a few more items, and a bottle of Jameson, before we resume the drive to my cabin. The flurries continue their dance with the ponderosas as soft Christmas music hums from the radio.

"Do you live here full-time?" My elbow rests on the back of the seat, fingers curled in my hair as I turn my body in his direction.

Jonathan shakes his head. "Not exactly. I have a place in Sutton, but I prefer it up here. It's quieter."

His eyes never leave the road, and mine never leave his face. He has secrets, and I find myself wanting to unravel them all, like a kid unwrapping Christmas presents. But I have a feeling if I push, he'll shut down.

And I'm running out of time.

"How long have you lived in Sutton?"

"You ask a lot of questions."

I grin, even though he can't see it. "I'm a curious person by nature. Can't blame me for wanting to know a little about the man who hijacked my Friday night."

Huffing, he finally turns his eyes to me for a split second before returning them to the road. "Hijacked? I think a short walk through the grocery store was the least you could do after scaring away all my fish with your screeching earlier."

"There you go with the screeching comment again. I feared for my life during that whole ride, you know! Besides, *you* offered *me* a ride back home."

My cabin is still glowing dimly from the Christmas lights as we pull up, and I can't help but wonder how cold it is inside now that the fireplace has been dead for the last few hours. "Fucking firewood," I mumble under my breath.

Jonathan gets out of his truck before I do and makes his way over to the shed with the woodpile. I'm fascinated that this man, who keeps turning from hot to cool and back again in an instant, is now collecting wood in his arms and heading for my front door.

Skipping up the steps, I push the door open and step out of the way. He brings the pile over and places it off to the side of the hearth before heading back out to grab more, all without saying a word.

Before I can even think to help him, he's back, stacking the rest before throwing a few pieces into the fireplace. He grabs the long lighter on the mantel and lights the fire, using the poker to move the logs for the best flame.

"This should last you through the night and most of the day tomorrow," he finally says.

I'm leaning against the kitchen counter, unashamedly admiring him as he works. When he stands and turns to look at me, I swear his eyes darken a fraction. But a blink later, they look normal again, and I convince myself it's just a trick of the light.

Swallowing thickly, I ask before I lose my nerve. "Did you want to stay for a drink?"

My tone is lower and raspier than I intend. Needier. Not hiding the thinly veiled intentions in my offer even the slightest bit. I'm single. He's single. He's gorgeous, and I'm not that bad if I say so myself.

Jonathan sticks his hands in his pockets and

hunches his shoulders as though he's cold again. "I should get back. Still gotta grab the auger and my pole."

Embarrassed, I push off the counter, nodding my head frantically, and move for the door. "Yeah. Absolutely. Me too. Well, not with an auger and a pole, but…late night. Big day tomorrow."

His lips curl in like he's trying to hide a smile, but he starts walking my way as I hold the door open. "Have a good night, Evelyn."

"Yep, you too. Thanks for the ride! The car ride, that is…you know what I mean," I ramble at his back as he makes his way to his truck. "Merry Christmas!"

He doesn't reply as he climbs into his truck and pulls away. As soon as the taillights disappear, I slam the door and hang my head for a second before going to grab a cinnamon roll. Once I have two reheated on a small plate, I pour myself a glass of pinot grigio–from a box 'cause I'm classy like that–and sit on the couch in front of the roaring fire.

Shoving half a roll in my mouth, I take a sip of my wine. Even though the temperature in the cabin is rising quickly, I wrap Jonathan's jacket around me and burrow further into the couch.

"Shit. He forgot his jacket," I mumble. Sitting back up, I start to shrug out of it before I stop. There's no way he didn't realize I was still wearing it. He was staring right at me before he walked out.

A small smile curls my lips up as I finish my rolls and glass of classy vino. Maybe Jonathan wants to see me again? Why else would he have let me keep his jacket? He did say I look like Barbie. Or, at least, I think that's what he said, anyway.

Maybe I wouldn't have to spend the Christmas weekend alone. Perhaps he and I could spend it together. I could unwrap all his secrets *and* him.

Whoa, there. Down, girl. You just met the man.

As I think about all the possible ways I could show up at Jonathan's house the next day, and all the things I could say, I stretch out on the couch and use his jacket as a blanket. My eyes grow heavy as I watch the firelight dancing on the walls—the oranges and yellows swaying to their own rhythmic rhumba.

chapter four

Lake Town is silent at nine in the morning. Its streets are covered in a fine layer of powdery snow, devoid of people. Christmas lights on the buildings are still lit up, casting a warm glow over the town. I can easily see myself living here, if I wasn't so set on traveling the world.

There are people in the coffee shop across from the grocery store Jonathan took me to last night–the only sign of life this early in the day. The morning chill is crisp and harsh as I make a beeline for the cafè, pulling Jonathan's coat around me as I walk.

By the time he gets it back, my Warm Vanilla Sugar body spray from Bath and Body Works will be ingrained in the heavy material.

Lake Town Lattes is painted in big red letters on the large window that looks into the small space. A charming little bell chimes as I open the door, and four sets of eyes hone in on me as the chatter quiets down. Three ladies that look to be in their sixties or seventies turn in my direction, their card game forgotten on the table they occupy in the corner of the shop.

Another lady is behind the counter and greets me with a warm smile and a cheerful, "Good morning, miss. What can I get for you today?"

Hushed murmurs begin as I walk to the counter. I send the ladies a small smile before turning my attention to the woman who spoke to me. "Good morning. I'd like a peppermint mocha breve, please."

"Sure thing, sweetheart," she says, turning slowly to start making my drink. "Haven't seen you around here before. Are you up for the weekend?"

"Yeah. I'm staying at the cabin on Rookford Drive."

One of the ladies in the corner cuts in loudly, "Oh, the one right across from Jonathan's place!"

My cheeks burn at her exclamation, and I wonder if they know the jacket I'm wearing is his. "Yep. Met him yesterday, actually. Quite the comedian, that one."

I'm met with a beat of silence before all four ladies break out in laughter. "Jonathan is the furthest thing from any comedian I've ever seen," one of them says.

"Well, can you blame him? After that tragic accident-"

"Hush, Elsie! It's not your place to be touting Jonathan's business everywhere," the woman behind the counter barks. She turns back to me and says, "That's Elsie. She's the town's biggest gossip. The other two with her are Judy and Esther. And I'm Clarice, but everyone calls me Cee."

Whatever Elsie had been about to say about Jonathan, I want to know. But the ladies have already gone back to their card game, murmuring amongst themselves in tones too low for me to hear.

"Jonathan is a good man. Don't let his gruff demeanor scare you. A big ol' teddy bear that one is." Cee brings my drink over and sets another next to it with a stopper plugged into the top of the to-go lid.

"What's this?"

She smiles and nods to my jacket. "One for Jonathan, dear. Tell him we say hello."

My cheeks warm again, and I dip my head in acknowledgment as I hand her a twenty-dollar bill. "Thank you, I will. I'm Evelyn, by the way, but my friends call me Evie."

"Well then, Evie. Enjoy your day. It's going to be a beautiful one. Nice time for a hike up to The Point, if you ask me. Wish I could still roam the mountains, but these knees aren't what they used to be." Cee smiles as she sets my change on the counter and turns to join the other ladies at the table.

I leave the money. Feeling as though her words are purposeful, I wonder what Point she's talking about. I love to hike, though, and have a feeling that perhaps Cee said something because Jonathan likes to do it as well.

As secluded as it is up here, I have a little bit of a difficult time finding the driveway to Jonathan's. Last night it was almost dark by the time we left, and I didn't catch the name of the street he lives on. So it's almost nine-thirty by the time I turn off my car and steel myself to knock on his door.

His drink is warm in my hand–my black, fingerless, Merino wool gloves, forgotten in the passenger seat in my haste to force myself out of the car before I could talk myself out of it. I walk slowly toward the house, muttering to myself about how best to ask if Jonathan wants to spend the day together. "Hey, I was just wondering if you….no. Good morning! Wanna go for a hike? No, that's fucking weird. This is all fucking weird, Evie. Hi, Jonathan. Cee said it was a nice day to go up to The Point. I have no clue what that is, but I want you to take me!"

"I'm not going up to The Point today," his smooth tenor breaks through my monologue.

"Ahh! Jesus Christ!" Startling, I spin to see him standing next to my car with a pile of wood in his hands. I'm thankful there's a stopper in his cup lid because if there hadn't been, his drink would be all over me. There's a small woodshed behind him, something I overlooked while driving. But I'll bet he saw me coming the second I turned in.

"What are you doing here, Evelyn?" His voice is rougher now, gritty, and his tone rakes down my body, heightening my senses.

After a moment, I raise my hand with his drink. "This is actually from Cee, not me. I came to return your jacket. But then she mentioned The Point, and I like to hike, so I figured that maybe you'd like to join me."

"You don't look like you came to return my jacket. In fact, you seem quite at home in it." He brushes past me, and the unmistakable scent of whiskey drifts off him in waves. Following, I pick up my pace so that I can open the door to his house since his arms are full.

"And you smell like a distillery. What did you do last night? Drink that whole bottle of Jameson?"

He stops right outside the open door, staring down at me with his hard, cold eyes, jaw clenching as our staring contest continues. But I refuse to back down. He doesn't intimidate me. Jonathan must realize this because eventually, he concedes, shaking his head before walking into the house.

This time he doesn't slam the door in my face.

Despite the way *he* smells, the inside of his house smells like apples and cinnamon and pine needles–like Christmas.

A fire roars in a large fireplace with a rustic stone hearth. The walls are colored a warm, glossy pine, and there are stone accents everywhere. It's an open concept, and as I move deeper into the house, I notice a large kitchen and a smaller den on the other side of it. There's a chunk of the steak he bought last night sitting out on a plate next to the stovetop as if he was getting ready to make it for breakfast.

Setting his drink on the tall counter that acts as a breakfast bar, and separates the kitchen from the living room, I hop on a stool and watch as he stacks the wood next to the fireplace. The Jameson bottle is sitting on a small coffee table in front of a worn, camel-colored sofa. It's nearly half empty.

"So, I guess I interrupted your breakfast…" I trail off.

Jonathan doesn't fill the silence that follows, but my stomach does—with a loud rumble as if to say, *"Great timing. We're starving."*

My hand flies to cover it as I suddenly find a random spot on the wall interesting. When I finally look at him again, he's scrutinizing me with thinly veiled annoyance. "I'm beginning to think you're very adept at interrupting meals in general."

"Hey, it's not like I *meant* to interrupt your fishing last night." Is it getting hot in here? Or is it just the way he's looking at me? He looks annoyed, but there's something else in the depths of his eyes. Like a fish swimming just under the ice-covered surface of the lake outside.

Jonathan shakes his head, breaking our eye contact as he walks into the kitchen. He grabs his drink off the counter, pulling the stopper from it before taking a large gulp and turning one of the burners on. There's a pan sitting on the back burner, and he moves it to the front after adding a little butter to it.

Spinning on the stool, I shrug out of his jacket and lay it on the seat next to me before propping my elbows on the counter. "So, if you won't take me to The Point, will you at least tell me how to get there?"

He doesn't look at me as he swirls the butter around in the pan. "You're not going out there by yourself. It's not safe."

I fight the urge to roll my eyes and say, "*Okay, Dad.*" Instead, I shrug and tell him, "Well, I don't want to spend the day cooped up inside. Cee is right. It's a beautiful day! Might as well get out and enjoy the fresh air!"

The sizzle of the steak hitting the pan makes my stomach clench again, and I hope it drowns out the pathetic song my hungry stomach sings. Was I supposed to grab something to eat at the coffee shop? Yes. But then I got distracted by what Elsie said about Jonathan and a tragic accident, and I forgot all about how my stomach was hungry for something besides cinnamon rolls.

"And do you have a gun?" he asks as he cracks eggs into another pan.

My brows shoot up to my hairline. "A gun? No! What? What kind of question is that?"

"A sensical one if you're planning on hiking in the mountains by yourself. There are mountain lions and moose–"

"A moose isn't going to attack me! Mountain lions, I get. But also, I hate guns. And killing animals for no reason. That's *their* home I'm walking in."

"A moose will absolutely attack you if you come up on it unexpectedly. And they blend in with the trees. Do you even know what to do if a moose charges at you?" He finally tears his eyes away from the stove and gives me a look that says he knows I don't.

Shaking my head, I raise an eyebrow and motion for him to continue. He flips the eggs in the pan like an expert, then turns the burner down for the steak. "If a moose charges you, get behind a tree. Preferably a big one. It's hard for them to maneuver around quickly, and they will most likely leave you alone once you've put something solid between you."

"Okay, sounds easy enough. As for the mountain lion, I'll take my chances. After all, my entire next year is going to be full of dangerous adventures. Might as well just get a jump on it now."

After a few minutes, Jonathan moves the steak to a plate as I slide off the stool, leaving his coat on the other one as I turn toward the door. "Thanks for the jacket. And you're welcome for the coffee, or whatever it is Cee made for you."

"Where are you going?"

"I told you, I wanna be outside."

"You don't know where you're going." He sounds amused, and it's a nice change from the annoyance that usually drips from his lips.

"That's what Google Maps is for," I say over my shoulder before tossing him a smirk.

He heaves out an exasperated sigh. "Sit down, Evelyn."

Oh, great. The annoyance is back. That didn't take long.

"You're not the boss of me." I sniff.

"Sit. *Down*. Evelyn," he repeats in a darker tone.

It's full of promises. Of deeply delicious things that I want to experience from him, and that thought makes me pause.

Turning, I see that he's not even looking at me but at the steak as he cuts half of it up into small pieces. There are two plates in front of him, both with two fried eggs that look like they're cooked over-easy. He puts the solid piece of steak on one plate and sets the other on the counter where I had been sitting.

"Eat." He slices through his and pops a piece in his mouth before looking back at me.

Steak and eggs? You don't have to tell me twice.

Sliding back on the stool, I pick up the fork off the plate and spear a bite of egg and then some steak. It melts in my mouth, and I can't stop the moan that leaves my mouth as I hang my head back and savor the taste.

"You cut it up for me?"

Jonathan pauses, and I swear his cheeks grow red as he shakes his head slightly. "Sorry."

"Don't be. And thank you. You know, for sharing your breakfast with me."

"Don't worry about it." He turns away, and for a second, I fear he's going to retreat back into whatever cold shell he was in when I arrived. My eyes return to my plate before snapping to the glass of orange juice he sets before me. Reaching for it, I offer him a warm smile.

"So, are you saying there's a chance you'll take me to The Point? I mean, you told me you were all alone this weekend. So, unless you have better things to do?" Trailing off, I look at him expectantly.

Something that looks suspiciously like a smile tries to pull at his lips, but he tampers it down and settles on a smirk. "I suppose I *would* feel pretty bad if you tried to go on your own and got eaten by a mountain lion."

"Yay!" I clap my hands together and flash him a toothy smile. He looks taken aback by my outburst, and I instantly stop clapping to pick my fork up again. "It will be fun. Besides, it's Christmas Eve. No one should be alone on Christmas."

Jonathan lets out a low hum of agreement, and I look up to see his gaze lost in the fireplace as he absentmindedly runs the fingers of his right hand over the ring finger on his left.

chapter five

$\mathcal{J}$onathan follows me in his truck as I drive back to my cabin. He says it will be easier to drive to the trailhead together, and I want to continue spending time with him, so I don't argue. I leave my keys on the counter and grab my bag of jerky, stuffing it in the deep pocket of my shacket.

His truck appears in the driveway just as I close the front door behind me. I can see him shaking his head at me as I get in the passenger seat, and I shoot him a quizzical glance. "What have I done now?"

"It's too cold today for whatever *that* is," he says, sending a judgmental look toward my shacket. As he puts the truck in reverse, he reaches into the backseat and pulls his heavy black jacket over the seat, tossing it in my lap.

"Aww, you fed me breakfast, and now you're clothing me! Cee was right about you. You may seem gruff, but inside, you're just a big teddy bear, aren't you?" I coo.

The truck comes to an abrupt halt as he slowly turns to look at me, less than amused. "Cee said that?"

My smile never falters as I hold his gaze. "Face it, Jonathan. You're stuck with me for the next few hours. You might as well *try* and lighten up a little."

He huffs and starts to drive again without saying anything. I let him have his silence and focus on the landscape as we venture past Lake Town for about ten minutes. The road we pull onto is hidden. One of those *if you don't know it's there, you'll miss it* type roads that makes me think The Point is more of a hike for locals and not for tourists.

"So, how far is the hike?"

"Depends. How good of a hiker are you?"

"Decent, actually. I hiked a lot before I got married." Out of my peripheral, I see him look at me for a moment before turning his attention back to the road.

"Ex-husband not much of an outdoors guy?"

"Yeah, no. Steven has no desire to be outside. He works a lot. It was part of our problem. He never had any time for me, and I gave up the things I loved so I could have dinner on the table when he got home." Resentment laces my tone. As much as I'm happy to be rid of the asshole, the situation still pisses me off.

Jonathan is quiet for a while before he says, "Four hours. If you're a decent hiker, it should take us four hours."

"There or round trip?" The jerky I brought wouldn't be enough to sustain me for an eight-hour hike.

As if he knows my thoughts have strayed to food, he laughs. It's loud and genuine, and brings a smile to my face. He slows the truck and pulls into a small area that looks like it's for parking. There's no one else here, and the snow is undisturbed, just as it was the whole road in.

"Round trip. Don't worry. I figured you didn't have a pack. I brought an extra with water *and* snacks." He grins at me, changing moods faster than the flip of a light switch. It's almost like he *wants* to be happy but then reminds himself to be grumpy instead.

The snow doesn't reach the tops of my Adirondacks as I get out of the truck. Making my way over to his side, I slip into his jacket as he pulls two black Camelbak hydration packs out and hands one to me. It smells like crisp pine–the air–in the way that only fresh snow in the forest can smell. Inhaling, the cold seeps into my lungs, and I'm glad for the thick winter headband I grabbed when I went into my cabin to get my shacket.

Sunlight beams down, reflecting off the snow causing the trail to glitter all around us while we walk. The only sounds are the snow crunching under our feet, the birds in the trees, and, every now and then, the wind whipping through the branches. There are no signs of wildlife other than the birds.

Eventually, I lose track of how long we've been walking, and I can't stand the silence anymore. "It's so beautiful up here. I'm surprised my dad never brought us up this way. We used to camp a lot when I was growing up."

Surprisingly, Jonathan keeps up the conversation. "Oddly enough, I didn't know this place was up here either. I looked for a cabin like mine for a while, and then one day, the listing was just there. My realtor and I never even met with anyone. It was all done electronically. Woulda thought it was a scam if all the paperwork hadn't been so legit."

He bends a snow-covered branch out of the way and steps back so I can pass him. I don't make it more than a few steps, though, before I feel him tug on the back of my jacket. "Let me stay in front. The last thing we need is a mountain lion coming straight at you. You'd probably try to pet it and call it a *pretty kitty.*"

"No, I wouldn't," I grumble while inwardly telling myself, *yes, you absolutely would.*

His lips are turned up in a grin as he passes me. He doesn't make a big deal of it, but he's dragging his feet as he walks so that the path is more clear for me. It's all the little things that are adding up that make me think there's so much more to him than he wants to let on. Sharing his breakfast, agreeing to go on the hike with me so that I'd be safe, bringing me his jacket and an extra Camelbak.

"So, tell me something about you, Jonathan. Anything you want." Getting him to open up was gonna be about as easy as opening a pickle jar. But I have a feeling that if I just bang his lid with a prover-bial knife, he'll pop open and let me enjoy what he has to offer inside.

"I like my solitude," he says under his breath.

"And why is that? What's a handsome man like you doing out here all alone? Hiding from the police? Ooh, do you have a gambling problem? Are you hiding from loan sharks?" I'm watching his feet as we walk, but he stops so abruptly that I run straight into his back.

"Evelyn, you are a very odd woman," he says over his shoulder before resuming his pace.

Even though he can't see me, I grin up at him with a silly face and laugh as I singsong, "And I think you could use a little oddness in your life,

Jonathan. And that wasn't an answer, so which is it? Loan sharks or police? Or maybe you're a serial killer, and you like to bring your victims out here!"

I'm ready this time as he whirls around, jumping to the side of the trail and bounding around him. Laughing, I bend to scoop some snow into my palm, rolling it into a ball as I watch an amused look cross his face. "If you're gonna kill me, you gotta catch me first."

"Evelyn, I'm not a serial killer. Besides, *you* were the one who wanted to go on this particular hike, remember? Put the snowball down." He places his hands in the pockets of the jacket he's wearing. It looks like his black one, only sand-colored, matching the beanie he's wearing.

"That's what a serial killer *would* say!" My eyebrow raises as I toss the snowball between my hands.

"Evelyn." He takes a lazy step toward me.

"Put." *Step.*

"The." *Step.*

"Snowball." *Step.*

"Down." He's nearly to me. His gaze darkens, and his lips tilt playfully.

Frozen, like a deer caught in headlights, I think about whether or not to throw the snowball–like prey trying to decide if it can outrun its hunter. "What are you gonna do about it if I don't?"

"You don't want to find out." He pulls his hands from his pockets slowly, fingers raised, as if not to scare me.

A thrill rushes through me. He's having fun, and I don't want this moment to end. So I do what anyone else would do in my position.

I throw the snowball in his face, turn, and start running like I'm being chased by Jason from the Friday the 13th movies. A snowball passes over my shoulder, making me jump as I let out a high-pitched squeal and laugh, trying to keep my balance now that I'm running in ankle-deep snow.

"Evelyn, get back here!" Jonathan yells behind me. Glancing back, I notice he's running after me but not as fast as he could be going. He's chasing, but letting me stay out of reach. There's a smile on his face, cheeks glowing red, and there's a silver glint in his eyes. He's painstakingly beautiful, and that thought makes me stumble.

Catching myself, I scoop some snow and toss it over my shoulder before picking up my pace, even though my lungs are burning from the cold air. I have no idea where I'm going, but continue to run between the trees. "Come on, slowpoke!"

"Evelyn, stop!" His voice is sharp and no longer playful. "Stop!"

Slowing my pace, I turn to look at him but only catch his eye for a split second before I'm suddenly falling. Letting out a short, piercing yelp, I tumble down what I hope is a hill and not a cliffside. Before I can let out another cry, I come to a stop, landing on my back. Snow creeps into my collar, the cold, wet slush sliding down into my shirt and seeping into my doubled-up leggings.

Jonathan is frantically yelling from above, and I raise my hand, giving him a thumbs-up. "I'm okay!"

Lifting my head, I can see him coming down the hill in a rush, trying not to fall. Rolling over, I stand and turn to him when he trips at the last moment and crashes into me. Suddenly, I'm on my back again, but instead of the sky, I'm staring into his eyes.

Breathing heavily, I manage a small, "Hi."

"Hi," he replies softly. "Are you okay?"

"Mmhmm. I'm good. What about you?" There are layers and layers of clothing between us, but I can feel the heat radiating off of him like he's my own personal Mylar blanket.

"I'm fine. Are you always this prone to accidents?" Smirking, he tilts his head and brings an arm up to rest next to my face.

Flashing him my pearly whites, I shrug the best I can. "Not really. It must just be something about *you.*"

I'm rewarded with a genuine smile, and my hand lifts to ghost my fingers across his lips. His breath is warm against my fingertips, and I desperately want to feel his lips on mine. "You have a really nice smile. You should do it more often."

He doesn't respond, his smile faltering as I drop my hand. Slowly, it feels like the space between us is diminishing. It takes me a moment to realize that his head is lowering, and I angle mine up as the heat from our bodies melts the snow around us.

It's almost the perfect moment, but just before our lips touch–right as I'm closing my eyes–Jonathan jerks back suddenly as if he's been burned. Guilt spreads across his face as he sits back on his knees before he stands, and I scramble up after him.

Clearing his throat, he won't meet my eyes as he motions further down the hill. "The trail keeps going that way–it's a switchback down the hill, but you kinda just eliminated the first part." He offers a quick upturn of his lips before serious Jonathan returns. And he pushes past me as if we hadn't almost just shared a kiss.

♡ ♡ ♡ ♡

The rest of the hike to The Point is painstakingly quiet. Every time I try and talk to Jonathan, he either just grunts in confirmation or gives clipped answers. It's like every time we take a step forward with his surly attitude, he runs two steps back.

My thighs burn as we ascend to the top of the steep mountainside. I chew on the bite valve of the crux reservoir, wishing it was a peppermint stick instead. It's been a while since I've climbed a mountain, but the view when we finally reach the summit is stunningly gorgeous.

Trees stretch for as far as my eye can see, all snow-capped and glittery against the azure sky. Further away, other mountains and bodies of water twine between them, while a small lake is nestled in what I assume is a glade down below the other side of the mountain. Its water isn't completely frozen, and the sun bounces off the shimmering surface.

"So beautiful," I murmur as I take it all in.

"It really is," Jonathan agrees.

Stealing a glance at him, my heart softens as I see how peaceful he looks. His head is tipped up to the sky, eyes shut, while the sun bathes his face. "It's moments like this that make me want to travel the world," I sigh wistfully.

His eyes open, and I look away quickly so he doesn't catch me staring at him. "You were serious about your eat, pray, love thing?"

"As serious as a heart attack. I want to see all the world has to offer, you know? Life is too short to waste it away, working yourself to death. Or to always be worried about things like retirement. People always say they have so much they want to do when they retire, but what if you can't at that point? What if you can't backpack through Europe? Sit on a plane for long enough to get overseas? What if your body breaks down and you physically just can't do anything? What a tragedy that would be." My eyes continue to roam the scenery, but I can see Jonathan looking at me from my peripheral.

It's a while before he says anything. "One of my biggest regrets in life is working too much."

He doesn't explain what he means, and I don't ask for him to elaborate even though I want to. I'm lost in my thoughts when a silver wrapper appears in front of my face. Blinking, I refocus to see Jonathan trying to hand me a protein bar. It's already unwrapped halfway, and I look over to see him eating his own, patiently waiting for me to take mine.

"You know, Jonathan. You're just as odd as I am. You're prickly, but you have these soft moments that make me feel like you weren't always so gruff. You're a natural caregiver." Taking a bite, I peek sideways to find him staring at me with a pensive gaze.

"Or maybe you just get off on treating women like children. There's gotta be a name for that type of kink. You do seem to enjoy feeding me," I muse, munching happily on my snack, my lips pulling up into a grin.

He shakes his head and turns to start his way back down the mountain. "Odd. Odd. Woman." I hear him utter mirthfully.

chapter six

Jonathan and I make small talk the rest of the way back. No mountain lions try to steal the bag of beef jerky we share. We do see two moose, but they have no interest in us.

As soon as we get back into the truck, Jonathan pulls some mini candy canes from his coat pocket and sets them in the seat between us with a crooked grin. Grabbing one, I beam and tear open the wrapper, sticking the end in my mouth. "Aww, Jonathan! See? Caregiver. Maybe I'll just stay at the cabin forever if it means you'll keep feeding me."

He chuckles as we start down the road. "Dear God, I'll have to start working again. You'll eat me out of house and home."

"You could teach me how to fish? We could live off the land. Wait, could we? You can't really farm up here, can you? Guess you'll have to build a greenhouse. But just warning you, I don't have a green thumb."

It starts to snow again. Soft, fat flakes—as if the weather waited for us to finish our hike. The sun disappears behind thick, gray clouds, and Jonathan turns the heat up.

"We haven't even known each other for twenty-four hours, and you're already planning on moving in and starting a farm?" he jokes with another chuckle.

He's been making jokes since we summited the mountain, no sign of grumpy Jonathan anywhere in sight. It's been nice. The conversation has been easy, and our earlier near kiss hasn't made things awkward.

As much as I'd love to ride *his* peppermint stick, I'm happy to have someone to talk to and laugh with.

"Hey! I never said anything about animals! I was just thinking potatoes, some lettuce, and carrots. *Maybe* a dog or two. I've always wanted a dog." The stick breaks in half, and I pop the curved end into my mouth, rolling it around on my tongue.

Jonathan has his own, holding it by the loop as he sucks on the end. My eyes linger on his mouth, imagining what it would feel like if he was sucking on me instead.

"I've always wanted a beagle, so I could name him Bagel. I don't know why. I just remember thinking of it when I was a little boy and thinking it would be cool." He looks over at me and catches me staring at his mouth.

My cheeks flush crimson as I whip my head to look out the window. Heat courses through my body in embarrassment, and suddenly it's too hot in the truck. Shrugging out of his jacket, I toss it in the back-seat. "I want a big dog, so *you* can have a beagle, but I want a German shepherd or something equally as large. Something I can take hiking with me for protection without having to take a gun."

"Fair," he says simply, tone lower than it was before. I don't dare turn to see what's caused the change in his demeanor. There's still heat between my legs that I'm attempting to extinguish by pressing my thighs together without making it obvious.

Usually, I have better control of my body than this. But since it's been a long while since anyone besides myself has touched my most intimate places, I feel as if I could come just from Jonathan putting his hands on me.

Suddenly, the air is charged. Thicker. Little hairs on the back of my neck raise in awareness of Jonathan's eyes on me when they should be on the road. That thought causes me to turn and look at him. He *is* looking at me, but his eyes dart back to the road when mine meet his gaze.

Swallowing, I don't look away as I reach down

for another candy cane. He reaches over at the same time and our fingers brush, sending an electric shock up my arm. An involuntary gasp leaves my mouth as I look down. He hasn't moved his hand but is flexing his fingers as if he felt it too.

"Jonathan?" My voice is breathy and quiet as I prepare myself to ask, point-blank, if he wants to sleep together.

"Yes, Evelyn?" His voice is just as quiet as he glances over at me expectantly.

And just as I open my mouth to ask the question, my stomach lets out a loud gurgle.

He laughs, a loud, full-bodied laugh, as his eyes swing back to the road and his hand retracts back to the steering wheel. "You're *still* hungry, huh?"

Not knowing whether to be embarrassed or impressed that he's laughing like he is, I grab another candy and stick it in my mouth. Shrugging, I sigh. "I can't help it. I've always been this way."

"Where do you put it?! You're tiny." It's meant as a compliment, I think.

Laughing, I gesture to the large turtleneck under my shacket. "Baggy sweaters and doubled-up fleece leggings are deceiving."

I'm not fishing for a compliment. I'm comfortable with my body. I like food. If I have to deal with a soft tummy and a jiggle in my ass, I'm perfectly content with that.

"Stop it, you're gorgeous, and you know it."

Swoon.

He frowns as if he realizes what he's just said. It's almost like he withdraws into himself as he starts to think about something that takes him far away from the warm truck. Something about the way he's gone quiet again keeps any more words from leaving my mouth. Thankfully, it's only a few more minutes until he's pulling back into my driveway.

As the truck idles, he pulls his beanie off and runs a hand through his hair. He looks like he's struggling to find something to say, so I save him the trouble. "Thank you for going with me today. I had fun. Have a good Christmas Eve, Jonathan."

Grabbing a few candy canes from the pile, I quickly slip out of the truck. I'm nearly to the steps before I hear him get out as well. "Evelyn!"

Whirling around, I notice he's taken a few steps toward me but isn't coming any further. His chest is heaving. His features are painted with uncertainty. "Thank you for getting me out of the house today. I needed it."

A flicker of disappointment flutters in my chest as I give him a small smile. "Anytime you're up for company, you know where I live. Well, at least until Monday." I let out a small laugh.

His lips twitch as he plays with the beanie he's still gripping. He doesn't say anything, so I offer a small wave and turn to go into my cabin. I don't turn around again, and as I lean against the door once I'm inside, it's a few minutes until I hear him pull away.

♡ ♡ ♡ ♡

The cabin is a comfortable, roasty toasty. I've got a fire going both downstairs and upstairs. When I got back a few hours earlier, I'd promptly taken a hot shower and changed into a pair of sleep shorts and a camisole. After drying my hair, I slipped on some knee-high fuzzy socks and a long, open cardigan sweater.

Currently, I'm sipping a glass of my box wine and browsing through Instagram on my phone. As I'm scrolling absentmindedly, a picture of Steven, his girlfriend, and her kids appears. They are all standing in front of the Christmas tree we always put up, wearing ugly Christmas sweaters.

Fucking asshole.

Groaning, I quickly toggle to his profile and click *Unfollow*, then toss my phone to the side as I lean my head back on the couch. I debate whether or not I want to turn the TV on to find some trashy reality show to watch until I fall asleep.

Worst Christmas Eve *ever*.

A knock on the door causes me to jackknife into a sitting position, almost spilling my wine in the process. At first, I think I imagined it. That it was just the wind from the storm that's picked up outside.

But then the knocking resumes, louder, with purpose. Setting my wine down, I rush over to the door, pulling it open to see Jonathan standing there with two large brown paper bags in his arms. He doesn't wait for me to invite him in, but pushes past me as he mutters, "About time."

He's wearing his red and black flannel and dark jeans. There's snow in his hair, and he shakes it out after he tosses his keys and wallet on the counter. When he turns to look at me, he swallows whatever it is he's about to say as his eyes darken and immediately sweep down the length of my body.

"What are you doing here?" My eyes follow where his gaze is pinned to my fuzzy socks, and I roll them when a smirk turns up his lips.

"Cute," he says before his eyes roam back up my body. "I brought things to make dinner."

"Make dinner? Jonathan, you don't have to do that." I wrap my cardigan tighter around my body and cross my arms under my chest.

His eyes drop to the bags on the counter, and he nods once before starting to unpack them. "I know I don't have to. But it doesn't really make a lot of sense for us to be spending Christmas Eve alone when we could just spend it together."

It was normal, the way he said it. Like it was

obvious. And I wonder if he'd wanted to say something earlier when he dropped me off. A small smile forms as I go grab my wine from the coffee table in the living room.

"I guess you're right. So, what are we having for dinner, then?" Moving back to the kitchen, I grab a glass from the cabinet for the Jameson he pulled out from one of the bags. It's the one from his house, still half full.

"It occurred to me that I should have asked you what you wanted, but if I'm being honest, I didn't plan this until I found myself at the store instead of home after I dropped you off. So, I got a ham, potatoes–since you seem to be partial to those." He shoots me a smile. "Cranberry sauce. Canned, I'm afraid."

"I love canned cranberry sauce!"

"Yams, stuffing, and gravy," he finishes.

"Geesh, are we feeding an army?" Grabbing the fancy whiskey stone he's unpacked, I set it in the glass before reaching for the Jameson.

"Figured we could eat the leftovers tomorrow for dinner," he says as he starts to look through the cabinets. He turns the oven on to preheat while grabbing various dishes and kitchen tools for preparing the food.

A thrill goes through me at his words. My hand pauses in my pour before I look over at him and singsong, "Are we spending the rest of the weekend together, Jonathan?"

The cabin grows marginally hotter as he turns to me, potato peeler in hand. It's already a small kitchen, but with both of us in it, the space seems tighter and more intimate. Jonathan sets the potato down and picks up his glass before asking softly, "Is that okay?"

He doesn't break eye contact as he lifts the glass to his lips and takes a sip. He sets down the peeler and picks up my wine glass, holding it out to me. "I don't want to be alone this weekend. And I don't think you do either. For whatever reason, we were drawn together yesterday. And this past day is the most alive I've felt in a while."

As I take my glass from his hand, I clink it against his. "Then here's to the rest of the weekend, *whatever it may bring.*"

*L*aughter fills the cabin as runny mashed potatoes go flying through the air. "You put *way* too much milk in them!" Jonathan laughs as he attempts to stop the KitchenAid mixer.

"Okay, I vote we just add the yams to make it thicker. We can roast the marshmallows later for dessert." Turning to grab the dish of yams that are ready to go in the oven where the ham is reheating, I squeal when he snatches my hand out of thin air.

"You better not ruin my yams! You can eat your runny potatoes just the way they are!"

"Oh, come on! You can give up some of them!" He's still holding my hand as he gently pushes me against the counter opposite his beloved yams.

"Nuh-uh. Yams are my favorite. You will not sully them with your milky potatoes." He gives me a playful look that I return as I reach behind me for the mixing bowl.

His eyes track my hand and grow wide as I scoop some potato from it, yet he still doesn't let go of the hand that's now cradled between us. "Evelyn, don't you dare. Put the potatoes down."

"Remember what happened last time you said those words?" I reply saucily. Before he can move, I smear the food on his cheek, wiping my hand down beneath his chin. "Oops."

"Oh, you're dead," he chuckles lowly, reaching for the bowl.

Squealing again, I turn and try to break his grip on my hand, but he's quicker and smears a glob of the mix across my face and into my hair. We break apart, both laughing, and I reach for the cranberry sauce at the same time he grabs for his yams. I giggle as he very carefully scoops a small amount out. The time he wastes trying not to ruin them allows me the two steps it takes to close the distance between us as I throw the cranberry sauce at his chest.

He's wearing a white shirt, and he looks down at it incredulously before reaching for me. Catching me around the waist, he smears the yams across my nose and mouth as I squeal, "Not your precious yams!"

Breaking away, I run around the counter, careful to keep the mess in the kitchen. Reaching over to grab more potato slop, I fling it at him as he grabs a handful of cranberry sauce and throws it back. It makes me feel alive. Like I'm a little kid again having a food fight in the cafeteria at school.

Only, we're adults. And the next time he puts his hands around my waist, it's not to spread more food in my hair or across my skin. Our chests are rising and falling with our labored breaths, lips pulling up in grins as we take in the mess we've made on each other. Jonathan raises a hand to wipe my potato-soaked hair out of my face as I run my thumb across his cranberry-covered cheek and stick it in my mouth.

His eyes track my thumb and darken as it disappears between my lips. Hands tighten on my waist as he steps into me. "Evelyn?" His voice is low and husky.

"Yes?" Mine is just as low. Needy and hoarse.

"I wanted it, you know? Earlier. On the hill." He

doesn't have to explain for me to understand what he means.

His head starts to lower as I reply, "I did too."

The feeling of his hand cradling my jaw, his thumb sliding up my chin and pressing against my lips, has me opening my mouth ever so slightly. He slides it in, and I close my lips around it, sucking as he groans. Liquid fire rushes between my legs, and I can feel him harden behind his jeans as he presses me between him and the counter.

He hooks his thumb behind my teeth and curls his finger around my lower jaw, pulling me forward. Just as our lips are about to collide, the shrill ding of the timer goes off, signaling that the ham is ready. It causes me to jump, and he lets go of me with a jolt, stepping back without another word as he goes to get the offending meat out of the oven.

When he turns back around, though, the desire in his eyes is flaming. And as he reaches for me again, I jump up to wrap my legs around his waist, our lips finally meeting in a mix of cranberry-yam goodness.

chapter seven

Jonathan walks us from the kitchen to the living room as our mouths mold together. Tongues, twisting. Teeth, biting. It's raw and primal. My hands tighten in his hair as he lays me on the couch, in response to the way his fingers dig into my skin.

My hands drag his sticky shirt up his body, and we break our kiss so I can pull it over his head. His large palm slides up my stomach and under my camisole to cup my breast. Arching my back and pressing my chest into his hand, I roll my hips against his the best I can, desperate to feel him against me.

His lips skate down my neck, nipping at the tender flesh as he flicks my nipple with his thumb. "Is this okay?" he whispers against my skin.

"Fuck yes, it's okay. I need more." Rolling my

hips against his again, I'm rewarded by him pressing his bulge right against my center as he chuckles.

"Needy, needy, girl," he says as he lifts his head and raises his body from mine. Biting my lip as his hand runs down from my chest to the band of my shorts, I buck my hips into his fingers as he gently skims them over my center, making me feel like I'll combust at any given moment.

His fingers move to his jeans, popping the button and pulling down the zipper. Frantically, I reach down to help him out of them until he's lying on top of me in only his boxer briefs. Our lips find each other again as he rocks against me over our clothes. I'm soaked to the point it's almost embarrassing. But as his fingers move to rub me over my shorts, he hums in approval before sliding his hand beneath the band.

"I don't have any condoms," he says against my skin. Pulling my camisole down with his teeth, he licks back up my breast to pull a nipple into his mouth.

"I'm clean, and I can't have kids if that's what you're worried about. But I swear to God, Jonathan, if you don't touch me, I'm going to die," I moan as his fingers freeze just above where I desperately want them. My leg hitches up as he slowly drags his fingers down to rub my aching bundle of nerves before dipping lower through my core to gather the arousal there.

"So fucking wet, Evelyn. Tell me, were you this wet on the hike? Did you walk through the forest with a mess between your legs?"

"Yes," I admit, turning my head to the side as he nips at my nipple again while pushing two fingers inside me.

Gasping, I clench my inner walls around them, hips undulating against his hand. Pulling mine from his hair, I reach down to cup him through his briefs, running my palm against the length of him.

"Shit." He sucks in a breath as his hips jerk at my sudden touch. Pulling back sharply, his mouth and hands leave me as he grips my shorts and under-wear, yanking them down my body. My cardigan is pooled at my elbows, having fallen off my shoulders earlier in the kitchen.

We're both breathing heavily as I watch him stare down at my bare pussy. His hand goes to his cock, fisting it through his briefs before he stands from the couch to pull them off. His length is thick and heavy, bobbing as it's released from its confines. Licking my lips, I can't decide if I want it inside me or if I want to taste it first.

"I'm clean too. It's been…a long time since I've been with anyone," he says.

Swinging my legs off the side of the couch, I sit

up and shrug out of my cardigan. Our eyes meet as I reach out, pulling him to sit down as I move to my knees and settle between his.

"Evelyn." His tone is hard and warning, as if he's not sure.

Dragging my eyes up his muscular body, I shrug slightly and wrap my hands around his shaft, relishing the air he sucks between his teeth. "What? I'm hungry," I say with a lilt, smiling coyly.

He throws his head back with a groan as I wrap my lips around his crown, flicking my tongue against the salty slit. Wrapping a hand in my hair, the other cups my cheek as he looks back down at me. "I do love feeding you," he says huskily.

Hollowing my cheeks, I take as much of him into my mouth as I can, swirling my tongue and coating him in my saliva. His hand twitches in my hair, and I have a feeling he wants to lift his hips to meet my mouth. Removing a hand from him, I reach up to squeeze the one on my head as I try to convey with my eyes what I want.

With the slightest pressure, he pushes my head down as his hips lift, and I smile around him, humming as he begins to fill my throat. I've always prided myself on not having much of a gag reflex. Not that I *try* to deep-throat phallic-shaped foods, but I chalk it up to my love of food and the fact that I usually stuff my mouth when I eat.

"Fuck, you're incredible. I wish you could see yourself the way I see you right now, taking my cock as good as you are. I'll build you a million greenhouses if it means you'll suck me off like this every fucking day."

Oh, Jonathan is a dirty talker. And *fuck*, it's hot.

My bare pussy clenches as my thighs are flooded with arousal at his words. Both of his hands are on the back of my head now, his hips moving faster as he fucks my face. Saliva starts to pool out of my mouth, and my eyes begin to tear, but I shake my head when a look of concern crosses his face. My hands tighten around him, twisting over the length I can't fit in my mouth.

"I'm going to come, Evelyn. And as much as I want to do it down your throat, I want to be inside you." He pulls my head off him and leans forward to tug me onto his lap.

His eyes immediately go between my legs as he licks his lips. "Are you sure?"

"Just fuck me already, Jonathan," I command, reaching down to position him at my entrance. Slowly, our eyes lock as I slide down, inch by slow inch, until I'm seated fully on his lap. I feel impossibly full, stretched to the point it's almost painful.

My body relaxes, though, as he slides his hands up to cup my breasts, leaning forward to kiss between them before licking a trail up to suck at the hollow of my neck. With each roll of my hips, my clit presses up against him, and I selfishly chase that feeling as I throw my head back in ecstasy.

"You feel so fucking good, so much better than I imagined," I whisper to the ceiling.

"You'll have to tell me all the things you imagined me doing to you. I'm going to make sure they all come true," he replies, driving his hips up as he reaches down to press his thumb to my clit.

Crying out, I pick up my pace, grabbing the back of the couch to give me leverage as I start to bounce up and down on his cock. "This is a good fucking start," I manage in a hoarse whisper.

"That's right, baby. Come for me." He pinches my nipple and rubs furiously at that spot between my legs as I drop my lips to his and cry my release into his mouth.

Biting his lip as I ride my climax, I love the sound of the strangled moan he lets out as he comes just moments after me.

My body sags against his, and I lay my head on his shoulder, his hand coming up to stroke my hair as he runs his fingers in circles against my hip. Neither of us say anything for what seems like forever, and part of me is worried that he may retreat back into himself now that we've given in to our carnal desires.

But his touches never slow. He makes no move to get up from the couch or to remove me from him. We both stay there, silent. The only sounds in the cabin are that of the roaring fire behind me.

That is until my stomach lets out a loud rumble. Followed by Jonathan's laughter.

After we dress, we bring what's left of the food to the living room and lay it out on the floor in front of the fireplace, picnic style. Neither of us bothering to get cleaned up, the promise of getting dirty again hanging in the air between us as we eat.

Taking a bite of his prized yams, I let out a moan and shake my head. "Okay, I totally understand why you didn't want to ruin these. I don't know how I'm going to live without yams like this from here on out."

Stretching out on the plush rug sans cardigan, Jonathan bunches up my camisole as he lays hot, open-mouthed kisses along my stomach, moving south. Chuckling, he reaches up and pulls the spoon from my mouth, and tosses it aside in the half-empty yam dish.

Continuing his journey, he pulls my shorts down, and I lift my hips to help him. Trailing kisses down my legs, he pulls off each fuzzy sock before hitching each one over his shoulders as he settles on his fore-arms. His hands loop around my thighs to pull them apart, and I look down at him as I run my hand through his hair.

It's easy now, the way we are with each other. Throughout the night, we've settled into this comfortable routine of eating, then engaging in sexual acts, and then eating some more. There hasn't been any more mood-switching for Jonathan. In fact, if I didn't *know* he was so moody before, I would never have believed that the man that's currently feasting between my thighs even *has* a moody side to him.

My legs fall open farther, hand tightening in his hair, as he starts to suck like he's trying to get a thick milkshake through a straw. I've never understood why men lick at you when they go down on you. It's all about the clit. At least, it is for me. All that other time is wasted. I don't need to be fucked with a tongue or have my lady lips played with. Just find that little golden buzzer and make it rain shiny confetti.

Jonathan knows exactly what I need without me even having to say anything, and for a moment, I think I'm willing to stay for a million greenhouses and to get *this* every day. My orgasm builds, and my body jolts as he scrapes his teeth gently against me. My free hand flies out to fist the rug, knocking against the yam dish.

The *only* thing that would make this moment better is…

"Don't even think about it," Jonathan commands. Sheepishly, I look down at him, my hand dropping from where it was outstretched toward my yam spoon. He flicks his tongue against my clit before he resumes building my climax. It doesn't take long before I'm coming, and he's drinking me down. My legs are boneless as he drops them from his shoulders and crawls back up my body, reaching for the spoon as he does.

"I feel like I'm dreaming. Like when I fell on the hill, I hit my head and haven't actually woken up, and this is all just my imagination," I say as he spoon-feeds me. It should gross me out to be spoon-fed like a baby, but it doesn't. Instead of giving me an ick, I feel taken care of.

Steven always said he was grossed out by my eating habits. And he absolutely HATED when I ate in bed or even on the couch. But Jonathan has made sure to give my soft tummy plenty of kisses and enough love nips on my dimpled thighs to show his appreciation for my body. And he genuinely seems to enjoy feeding me.

Is that a kink? I feel like that should be a kink.

"Mmm. Peppermint dreams," Jonathan murmurs against my lips.

"Peppermint dreams?" I giggle as he kisses me.

"You smell like peppermint, taste like peppermint–no matter what you eat or drink. I will forever associate peppermint with you," he explains.

"Mmm. More like peppermint wishes. I've been thinking about this since you dropped me off last night and brought wood inside for me."

He laughs in between slow kisses. I've lost count of how many times we've made each other come, and I have no clue what time it is. My body is deliciously sore, yet we're both still sticky from our earlier food fight.

As if he can read my thoughts, he pulls back and gets to his feet, reaching down to help me up. "Come on. We're overdue for a shower. Or a bath? I don't know what this place has."

"A bath sounds so lovely. Upstairs has a huge free-standing tub, but as much as I want a soak, I think a shower sounds better. The bathroom has a shower, too."

Slipping my shorts back on, I start to grab the dishes and groan as I remember we have a huge mess to clean up. "The hosts are going to give me such a bad rating if I don't find every speck of mess we made."

Jonathan shakes his head and waves his hand as if he's shooing away a fly. "Don't worry about that right now. Let's get cleaned up, and we can take care of it tomorrow."

A quick glance at the clock tells me it's two in the morning. We'd been so wrapped up in each other that we never even realized how late it was getting. Suddenly, I'm a little self-conscious. Is he planning on staying? Or is he going to leave me alone to go back to his cabin?

The fire has died down to embers, and I pull my cardigan on as Jonathan starts to spread them so they die out. When he's done, he turns to me and reaches for my hand. "Does this place have a washer and dryer?"

Nodding, I motion down the hall, where there's a half bath and a small stacked unit. "In there."

"Okay, why don't you go run a shower and throw your clothes down to me? I'll start a load while we get cleaned up."

"And what am I gonna wear to bed?" Raising my eyebrow, I tilt my head up to look at him with a saucy grin.

He captures my lips in a searing kiss as he pulls my cardigan down my arms. Then pulls back and says, "I guess we're both just gonna have to sleep naked tonight."

A smile lights up my face as he reveals his plans to stay the night, and I give him a light kiss before turning to go upstairs. He starts the laundry before joining me in the shower.

Steam curls around us like a peppermint infused

sauna. He runs my loofah gently over my chest as I lean back against him. He kisses my neck and I feel that ache between my thighs awaken again. "Jonathan…" My needy whisper bounces off the walls, louder than I intend, as his other hand moves lower.

He's thick and full against my butt, and I grind back against him as his fingers find that sensitive spot. He starts to work me while gently running the loofah over my nipples. My breathing intensifies as his fingers pick up speed. Reaching behind me, I flatten my palm against his length and grip him the best I can in our position.

A low groan fills my ears as he skims his lips up my neck and nips my earlobe, hips thrusting forward as his hand cups between my legs to push me back into him. The heel of his hand grinds against my clit as he lowers his lips again and sucks at the sensitive flesh where my neck meets my collarbone.

"Come for me, Evelyn. I want to hear my name on your lips when you do."

My hand tightens around him, the angle of my arm almost painful as he thrusts into my hand. But his fingers between my legs are magical and when he pushes two of them inside me, I cry out, "Jonathan, I'm gonna come!"

"That's right, baby. Say my name again while you ride it out."

"Fuck! Jonathan! Yes! Oh my God, yes!" My voice pitches into a hoarse cry as he continues to pump his fingers into me, grinding his hand against my clit, and just as my orgasm ends, I feel another one cresting.

"Fuck, Evelyn," he moans into my ear and I feel something warm hit my lower back and drip down between my cheeks.

Pulling back against him gently, he lays a kiss on my temple before he continues to wash me with the loofah. "I just can't seem to get you clean, without wanting to dirty you up again."

A giggle escapes me as I take the loofah and soap it up again, before I take my turn washing him. When we're done and dried off, he slips into bed and looks at me expectantly.

"I have to dry my hair. It's bad to go to bed with wet hair." Grinning at him when he gives me a pointed look, I plug in my blow-dryer and say over the noise, "I'll be quick."

By the time I finish, he's already fast asleep. So, I go back downstairs to get a glass of water and see that he cleaned up the dishes from the floor and smothered the embers in the fireplace before he joined me in the shower.

Creeping back upstairs quietly, I crawl into bed carefully so I don't wake him. In his sleep, he turns on his side and curls an arm around me, pulling me closer. It doesn't take long for slumber to claim me as well. Closing my eyes, I fall asleep to the thick scent of my peppermint body wash.

❤ ❤ ❤ ❤

The smell of bacon pulls me awake. Bacon and the Christmas music that's drifting softly from downstairs. Stretching under the covers, I wipe the sleep from my eyes and then remember I'm completely naked.

Sitting up, I immediately notice that my sleep set, fuzzy socks, and cardigan are laid out at the end of the bed on the side Jonathan slept on. Smiling, I grab them and get dressed. It's cold this morning, and as I come down the stairs, I can see Jonathan hasn't started another fire yet.

But he *is* cooking breakfast.

Pulling my long hair up in a messy bun, I slowly creep toward the kitchen, carefully trying not to alert him to my presence. My heart just about melts as I watch him, towel thrown over his shoulder as he poaches eggs and hums along to the Michael Bublé version of "White Christmas".

He's wearing a black shirt under a blue, white, and gray flannel, so I assume he left at some point this morning and came back with fresh clothes and more groceries.

"Good morning, gorgeous," he greets, startling me out of my thoughts.

My eyes snap up to his to see him smiling at me. "Good morning. How long have you been up?"

"I'm an early riser. Habit from when I worked in the city. You looked peaceful, so I didn't wanna wake you. I just ran over to my place to get some new clothes and grab some things for breakfast." He arranges the bacon on a toasted English muffin, before placing a poached egg on it, and spooning hollandaise sauce over the top.

"You made eggs benny?! Mmm, I'm starving!" Wasting no time, I pick up the fork he sets in front of me and dig in before he can even set the plate down on the counter in front of me.

Chuckling, he picks up a piece of bacon and bites off half the strip. "I figured you'd like a nice Christmas brunch."

Glancing at the clock behind him, I notice it's nearly noon. "Jonathan! You shouldn't have let me sleep so long!"

We only have until tomorrow together. Inwardly, I start to panic slightly at the realization that I wasted half a day sleeping when I could have been spending time with him. Irrational tears prick at my eyes, and I shake my head and wipe them away quickly so he won't see them.

But, of course, he does.

"Evelyn, what's wrong? Why are you crying?" Coming around the counter, he pulls me into his arms, and I start to laugh through my tears.

"I don't know. It's silly, isn't it?" I sniff and continue to wipe my eyes as he leans back and looks down at me.

"Is my cooking that bad?" The look he's giving me says he knows it's not his cooking that's caused my tears. Concern is etched across his features as he rubs his hands up and down my arms.

Playfully, I smack my hand against his chest and turn to my plate again. "Shut up. You know it's not your cooking. I'm just upset I slept through half the day."

He nuzzles my neck from behind and whispers in my ear, "Merry Christmas, by the way."

"Merry Christmas, Jonathan."

Cutting into my eggs Benedict, I take another bite as he rounds the corner to go back into the kitchen and turn the burners off, transferring the last of the bacon from the pan to a napkin-covered plate.

"I was thinking, after breakfast, we could take a nice long soak in that bath upstairs. I don't know about you, but that mountain did a number on my legs yesterday," he says as he fixes himself a plate.

Groaning at the thought of a hot bubble bath, I nod enthusiastically. "Yes, please! I'm so down for that."

We finish our breakfast, and I help him wash the dishes, realizing that our entire mess from last night has been cleaned up. "Did you clean everything while I slept?"

He laughs sheepishly, cheeks turning pink as he puts our plates away. "Yeah. I figured out of all the things I want to do with you before you leave tomorrow, cleaning up isn't one of them. At least not cleaning up the kitchen."

His tone is suggestive and causes butterflies to flutter in my stomach, their wings brushing my insides and sending tingles throughout my body. Jonathan leads me upstairs and starts to run the bath, and I grab my body wash from the shower and pour some of it into the water stream as it runs from the faucet. The smell of peppermint fills the bathroom again, and I turn to see that he's already stripped down and is stepping out of his boxer briefs.

Biting my lip, I quickly strip out of my clothes and follow him into the bath. He gets in first and offers his hand to help me, then he sits and pulls me down between his legs, my back to his chest, as he guides my head to lie on his shoulder. The bubbles are thick and minty, and he absentmindedly runs his fingers in lazy patterns on my skin as the hot water soothes our limbs.

It's been such a long time since I've been with anyone, that I'm sure my body is more sore from our coital activities than it is from the hike yesterday. "Tell me something, Jonathan. Anything. Something that you haven't told anyone."

His hand stills for a moment before he continues to trace my skin. Nuzzling his mouth to my ear, he whispers, "Christmas used to be my favorite holiday, but I haven't enjoyed it these past few years. This is the happiest I've been in a very, very long time."

A smile stretches my lips as I turn my head and give him a light kiss. "Same here."

The smile he gives me makes my heart skip a beat as I follow up with, "And to think, you were so grumpy when we first met."

My body vibrates with his full laugh as he leans his head back on the lip of the tub. "You weren't exactly a peach there yourself, sweetheart."

"Fair." Shrugging, I turn slightly so that I'm lying on his chest. The tub is huge, and since we're half-propped up, I can stretch my legs easily, tangling them with his.

"Why don't *you* tell *me* something?"

Thinking about what to share with him, I bring my hand up to curl against his chest. "I've always wanted to travel, but Steven–my ex–was more focused on growing a family. At first, I was fine with it because I wanted to have kids, too. But the longer time went on, the more we tried, the more we fought. He was so angry every time I–" My voice catches as my emotional past comes rushing to the surface. "Every time I miscarried. It was like he took it as a slight against him. At first, he was understanding, but...after the third time, he ran out of patience."

Jonathan's fingers tighten on me as he lifts his head. "I'm so sorry, Evelyn."

Shaking my head, I wipe away a stray tear that's falling down my cheek. "I wanted to take a break. Take a trip somewhere warm and try to stop feeling like I was a failure. But he wanted to do IVF instead. It was...horrible...for lack of a better word. I was always sick and moody. I finally begged him to let me stop. He started his affair the following week."

He tightens his arms around me and kisses the top of my head. "Jesus Christ. I don't even know what to say."

"This is the first time I've told anyone the full story," I admit softly. "All our friends were his first. My parents are dead. I haven't really had anyone to talk to. I thought about going to therapy but can't afford it. But I'm healing and looking forward to my next adventure. I'm selling my parents' house and going to travel Europe. I'm going to do all of the things that make me happy. That I've always wanted to do. Take my life back into my own hands. You know?"

He hums in agreement, lips pressed to the top of

my head as I tell my story. After a few silent minutes, he speaks. "My family is gone as well."

"Your parents?"

It's almost a full minute before he replies, "My wife and daughter."

The butterflies that had taken up residence in my stomach earlier transform into a feeling more like balls in a bingo cage. Heavy and uncomfortable as a breath leaves my mouth in a shallow gasp. "What happened?"

My thoughts stray to what Elsie had said about Jonathan and a tragic accident. This must have been what she was talking about.

"It happened two years ago, at Christmas. This time of year is…hard for me. We always used to spend Christmas with her family up North of the city, but I'd gotten a promotion at work, and I'd been there a lot. Pulling late hours and working weekends. They wanted me to work Christmas, and I agreed. Tiffany was so mad at me–that was my wife. And my little girl," his voice catches as he says her name, "Jenny was so sad. But I thought I'd have time. Plenty of other Christmases to spend with them. And I told her to just stay for one Christmas, but she didn't want to, so she and Jenny went. And they got in an accident."

Tears are falling from his eyes, and I reach up to cup his cheek, smoothing them away with my thumb as he continues. "Tiffany lost control on an icy patch of road. She hit someone else and flipped the car. She died on impact. Jenny passed in the ambulance on the way to the hospital."

He's trying not to break down, and I hug him the best I can in our position. He wraps his arms around me and buries his face in my hair as sobs rack his body. "Jonathan, I'm so sorry."

What he went through makes my shit with Steven seem so insignificant. I almost feel embarrassed by my confession when he was holding all of that in. Tears fall freely as he comes apart in my arms. It's no wonder his mood has been so hot and cold. He prob-ably feels guilty for feeling any sort of happiness after what happened.

"It's all my fault. I should have been with them," he cries.

Shaking my head, I pull back and cup his cheeks in my hands. "No, Jonathan. Don't say that. What happened to them is awful, but you can't blame yourself."

"Yes, I can. Jenny was only six-years-old. She had her whole life ahead of her. And Tiffany sacrificed her job to stay home and take care of her while I made a name for myself. I was selfish and put my dreams in front of them–"

"You were trying to take care of your family. There's a difference," I soothe. Our tears have stopped, but I can tell he's still worked up. Shifting carefully so that I don't splash water over the edge of the tub, I stand and reach for a towel to cover myself.

Once I'm out of the bath, I hand him a towel as he gets out as well, then I wrap my arms around him and hug him properly. "They wouldn't want you to keep living your life in isolation, punishing yourself for something you can't change."

He makes a humming sound against my hair as he hugs me back. "Thank you."

Pulling back, I smile up at him, and even though I'm slightly afraid to ask, I do. "Do you have pictures of them? I'd love to see them."

Smiling down at me softly, he nods. "Yeah, I do."

Once we're dressed, Jonathan drives us over to his cabin. I wait for him in his living room while he runs up to his bedroom and grabs a photo album. It's one of those old-school, thick, brown leather types. The ones like a three-ring binder that can hold hundreds of photos. And it's filled with photos of Jonathan and Tiffany from their early dating years, through their wedding, and the birth of Jenny. All of her big milestones, from her first steps to her first ice cream cone.

He shows me the necklace he had made for

Tiffany that Christmas. It's a pendant of platinum, diamond, and alexandrite–her birthstone and, ironically, mine as well–in the shape of the North Star. The chain is short and dainty, meant for the star to fit in the hollow of your throat.

My heart bursts with joy as I study years of Jonathan's life while he tells stories behind the photos. We spend the rest of the afternoon talking about the *good* times when Tiffany and Jenny, and my parents were still alive. Swapping stories and telling tales from our younger days.

When there's a lull in the conversation, I notice a sad smile crossing his face and reach out to cup his cheek, bringing his gaze to mine. "What is it?"

Shaking his head slightly, he lays his hand over mine and gives me a small smile. "Nothing. It's just…nice to talk about them with someone. Tiffany's parents…they don't speak to me. And I don't blame them, but sometimes it's like I wonder if that part of my life even existed. Does that make sense? It's been a year and a half since I've spoken their names to anyone."

Leaning over, I rest my forehead on his. "You can tell me every single story if you want, Jonathan. I'll listen to them all."

Letting out a laugh, he grips my hand against his cheek tighter and lays a chaste kiss on my lips. "It's like you're some sort of Christmas angel or something."

"Oh gosh, well *now* you've gone too far," I joke. "I'm certainly no angel. In fact, I think it's time for a drink." Standing, I pull him up with me. "Come on, let's go back to my place and get cozy and you can tell me all the things."

ack at my cabin, we settle in front of a fire, me with a glass of wine and him, his Jameson. Plates with leftovers cover the coffee table. This time we eat like normal and don't cover the cabin in food.

As night rolls around, he asks me a question that I'd never considered before. "What will you do when you come back from your trip? Why not keep your parents' house so you have something to come back to?"

"Honestly, I never really thought of that. But I haven't had a job in years. Steven always wanted me home to take as much stress off my body as possible. So I don't exactly have a lot of money. And my parents' home doesn't really *feel* like home anymore, you know? Sutton doesn't feel like home. So my plan is to sell the house and use the money to travel. If not now, when? This is the perfect time to go. I can do odd jobs along the way if I need to. As far as what I'll do when I get back, well, that is still to be determined."

He looks pensive and opens his mouth to reply, but then shuts it and doesn't say whatever it was he was going to. Part of me wonders what would become of us if I stay. Would he want to continue seeing me? Or did he get involved with me because he knew I'd be leaving tomorrow?

When I do go, I know I'll be leaving a part of me behind. Jonathan has awakened a side of me that's been dormant for a long time. He's made me feel wanted and cherished more in the last two days than Steven did in the last two years.

But two days is such a short amount of time. It's a fling. Perhaps the beginning of something more, but we don't have the time to explore it. Not unless I stay. My head and heart are at war with each other over that fact, like a proverbial angel and devil on my shoulders.

I can stay and explore this with Jonathan, that is, if he even wants me to. Or I can leave and not put my dreams on hold for a man again.

But there's the little fact that, again, it's only been two days. I don't want to come off as crazy and be like, *"Hey, I know we've only known each other for a weekend, but I really like you and think that maybe we should see where this goes."*

"What are you thinking so hard about over there?" His voice cuts through my thoughts like butter. Smooth and deep, in a tone I've come to recognize as meaning one thing—he has sex on his mind.

My eyes find his to see that he's moved closer to me on the couch, close enough that he reaches out and pushes a stray lock of hair out of my face before cupping my cheek and leaning in to lay a gentle kiss on my lips.

Gentle turns to an inferno as he pulls me into his lap and pries my mouth open with his own. He takes the wine glass out of my hand and leans us forward to set it on the table, never breaking our kiss. Then he stands from the couch, hands under my thighs as he carries me up the stairs to the bedroom.

My back bounces off the plush mattress as he goes to work, undoing the laces of my boots and pulling them off before removing my socks and leggings. Kissing up my legs, his long arms reach up to shove my sweater up my body, and I help by pulling it the rest of the way over my head. Once I'm nearly naked, he pulls something out of the pocket on his flannel, and I brace myself up on my elbows to see what it is.

Slowly, he grins as he brings a familiar white and red round candy to his lips, sucking it through its flimsy plastic wrapper. Heat courses through me as I wonder what he plans to do with the peppermint candy.

Hooking my legs over his shoulders, he reaches up and pulls my underwear down my legs, flinging them across the room. "I wanted to make our last night memorable," he says as he kisses his way from my knee to my inner thigh.

"How do you plan on doing that?" My voice is breathy as I watch him roll the candy against my skin before sucking the sticky flesh into his mouth.

"By doing something you'll, hopefully, never forget." Then his mouth closes around my already pulsating clit.

"Fuck," I cry as my elbows give out, and I fall back to the bed. Digging my heels into his back, I attempt to pull him closer as the mint from the candy sends a tingly sensation zipping up my spine. It's like every sensation has been heightened, and I throw my arm over my mouth to try and quiet my moans.

Jonathan chuckles against me as my other hand finds the top of his head, and I start to ride his face. It doesn't take me long until I'm coming undone, and as I'm still riding my high, he crawls up my body to drop the peppermint in my mouth.

There's something exotic about tasting myself on the mint as I roll it around on my tongue while Jonathan gets undressed. I plan on returning the favor with what's left of the candy, but before I can even move, he's pushing inside me. He slides in deep and pulls out slowly before repeating his movements at an agonizingly slow pace, like he's trying to savor the moment.

We kiss slowly, the mint growing smaller between our tongues. My skin is slick with sweat from the heat and our activities, and I look forward to another bath with him after this. His cock twitches inside me, a sign he's nearing his release, and he rolls over, pulling me with him until I'm on top. Pushing up till he's deep inside me, his hands pull my hips down as I rock them back and forth. Picking up my pace, he strokes that special place deep inside that has me coming undone after a few more minutes.

After we come together, I collapse on his chest for a moment before rolling off him. "Fuck, I'm going to miss this."

He looks at me sideways before moving to his side and reaching out to pull me in for another kiss. And I know, without a doubt, that if he asks me to stay, I will.

"I need to go take care of the fire," he murmurs against my lips.

"I'll come with you. I need to clean up the food anyway." Rolling over to grab my clothes, I let out a laugh when he grabs me around the waist and pulls me back down.

"You stay here. I'm not done with you yet," he says into my neck.

"Mmm. Yes, sir."

Grinning, he gets up and walks, naked, downstairs. There are noises of dishes clinking together, and I smile, knowing he's cleaning them for me. Stretching out on my stomach, I close my eyes for a moment and think about all the ways I could bring up staying and not seem like a crazy broad.

My breathing evens out, and I'm vaguely aware that my body is fighting sleep, waiting for him to return. Seconds stretch into minutes, and that line between lucid and dreaming grows blurry.

The last thing I remember is hearing Jonathan whispering a soft, "Merry Christmas, Evelyn."

chapter eight

It's eerily quiet when I wake.

Despite the quilt that's covering me, I can feel the chill in the air as consciousness creeps in. Reaching out for Jonathan so I can snuggle into his side and siphon his warmth, I frown when my arm is met with an empty space. It's cold, as if he left it hours ago. But there's no fire in the woodstove. No fragrant bacon wafting up from the kitchen.

Clutching the quilt to my naked chest, I call out for him. "Jonathan?"

Silence.

There's a stillness in the cabin I can't explain. Like when you're in the middle of the forest as it's snowing, and there's no sounds of nature—only your breathing.

Unnerving. Unnatural. Unwelcome.

My heart seizes as panic grips it in its ice-cold

hand. It's foolish, I know. He may have gone back to his cabin. Or out gathering wood.

Wrapping the quilt around me, I rise from the bed and go to the doors that lead out onto the balcony. It's snowing, not quite a storm, but it looks like it's gearing up for one. The clouds are fat and gray, the sky a gloomy slate. Flakes fall both vertically and horizontally in a chaotic dance.

There's no sign of Jonathan. His truck is gone from the driveway, its tracks filled in with snow. As if he were never here to begin with.

Disappointment sears through my chest like an ice pick to my heart. Why did he leave without saying anything? He knows I'm leaving today.

Blowing out a breath, I turn to check the time on the little digital clock on the nightstand. It's barely nine. The snow is too thick to see across the lake, so I can't tell if there's smoke rising from his chimney or if his truck is in the driveway.

Dressing quickly, I lace up my boots and head downstairs. They're unexplainable, the tears that prick my eyes as I reach for my coat and the keys to my car. There's still a few hours before I need to check out, and I desperately want to say goodbye to him.

My brain is screaming at me. *He left you. He doesn't want to say goodbye, or he would have been there when you woke up.*

Irrationally, I argue with myself that even though it's only been a little over two days, we connected emotionally. And that *has* to mean something.

As I start my car, another thought enters my mind. What if he just went to town for groceries? Or coffee? What if I'm not here when he returns? What will he think?

His tire tracks are long gone. He left too long ago for groceries or coffee.

Frantically, I put my car in drive and head toward his cabin. The road is icy, and though I'm careful, my tires slip in random spots the entire way. Wind whistles through the vents as it picks up and rocks my car. "Rockin' Around the Christmas Tree" plays quietly on the radio and I grab a candy cane from the passenger seat to suck on, keeping my teeth from clenching together in fear every time my car slides.

By the time I pull into his driveway, I'm upset to see that his truck isn't here either. There's no smoke billowing from the chimney, no lights on when I peek into the giant front windows. No answer at the door when I knock. There's also no tire tracks that give away any evidence that he's been home recently.

My hands grip the steering wheel as I drive into town. The roads are bare. I don't pass a single person on the way in, and multiple businesses have their signs flipped to closed as I pass through the small town. Cee and the ladies aren't in the coffee shop. Even the grocery store's parking lot is empty.

There's no sign of Jonathan's truck anywhere.

Turning around, I head to the only other place I can think to look. But when I pull onto the road that leads to the trailhead for The Point, passing it three times and having to continuously back up to find it, I'm dismayed to find no tracks leading down to the small lot. No vehicles. No footprints leading to the trailhead, even though the snow would have covered any that were left more than ten minutes ago.

Wind swirls the snow and continues to rock my car from side to side on the road as I go back to my cabin. The next hour is spent turning over everything to see if I missed a note from him.

But there's nothing.

No note.

None of his clothes, or even any evidence he'd brought groceries over to cook. The trash is gone, an empty bag in the can. Even my empty wine box is gone. The dishes have all been cleaned and put away. Everything in the kitchen looks exactly as it had when I'd arrived on Friday.

A sob tears through me and I shake my head furiously, as if trying to shake the sad feelings away. Deciding against starting a fire, I go upstairs and throw all of my stuff into my suitcase. There's no pausing to shower or bathe. Jonathan cleaned everything, so there's literally nothing for me to do, except pack my stuff up and leave.

So that's what I do.

♡ ♡ ♡ ♡

*H*ours pass with no sign of Jonathan.

After I left the cabin, I went to his again and decided to sit in the driveway to wait for him to return. At some point, maybe around the second hour, and the twentieth round of solitaire I'm playing on my phone, I think about going to see if the door is unlocked. Nature is calling, and that will just be a bright red cherry on a shit cake if he were to come home to me squatting in his driveway mid-stream.

Around hour three, I decide I can't take it anymore and run to the woods that surround his house to relieve my bladder quickly.

My stomach starts to gurgle at hour four. Candy canes do not a meal make.

With every passing hour, my dread grows as clarity sets in. Jonathan left without saying goodbye. He knew I was leaving today, and didn't care enough to give me a proper farewell.

It hurts.

It puts this weekend into perspective.

A fling was all it was to him.

We were both lonely and available. A good time for the weekend. An easy thing to let go of.

If it's so easy though, why does it feel like my heart has been crushed to pieces like the crumbs of peppermint candies at the bottom of their wrappers?

♡ ♡ ♡ ♡

The drive back to Sutton sucks. It's terrifying because of the road conditions, miserable because I'm in my feelings over the whole situation with Jonathan, and annoying because I can't stop my mind from replaying every little moment we had this weekend. Picking apart every look, every touch. Searching for something, *anything*, that would lead me to believe this had been his plan all along. Granted, it was me who'd pushed myself into his personal space, but he'd been the one to come back after dropping me off Saturday night.

Walking into my parents' house, I scrunch my nose at the offensive smell that is so strong I can taste it. It's starting to take on that musty scent that happens when no one has occupied a space for a while, the dust collects, and the air gets stale.

Throwing my suitcase on the floor in my childhood bedroom, it bangs against the hardwood, causing me to flinch as it most likely leaves a mark, but I don't bother to check. Instead, I flop down on my bed and groan as dust bunnies fly into the air.

Grumbling, I roll back off the bed and collect all of my bedding, taking it down the hall to the laundry room. After I start a load, I go downstairs into the basement to see what kind of canned goods are still edible.

The basement is filled with boxes of junk that my mother could never seem to get rid of, and I realize, with painstaking certainty, that it's going to be hard to get this place ready to sell.

Days fly by, though. Filled with people coming in and out of the house as I attempt to hold somewhat of a winter garage sale. It ends up being cathartic in a way. There's so much junk, but there are also so many memories. All the good ones, I box up and keep for storage, while all the bad get sold off for pennies on the dollar.

A little research and a few meetings was all I needed to select a realtor. Market value for the house is higher than I expect and she thinks it will sell fast. Part of me thinks back to what Jonathan said about keeping it, though, and I dabble with the idea of renting it out instead. At least while I'm on my trip.

All week my nights have been filled with McDonald's takeout and itinerary planning. Love has been dropped from my eat, pray, love mantra, and now I plan to just eat my way through Europe, Asia, and Africa.

And hopefully find myself again. Find the part of me that used to make me happy before Steven ripped my heart from my chest and stomped on it. Before Jonathan wrapped me in a peppermint scented cloud of lust and then promptly dissipated.

Google has not been my friend where he is concerned, either. With no last name, and no knowledge of his prior occupation, I'm not able to find anything online about Jonathan. There isn't anything about Tiffany or Jenny and their car accident either, at least not that I can find. The listing for the cabin I stayed at has been removed from Vrbo as well, so I'm not even able to get somewhat of an idea for an address to look up to see if I could get his information that way.

Full on stalker is what I'm turning into.

It's got to stop.

Sighing, I exit out of the window where I just booked a Goddess retreat in Bali. My credit card is already getting a workout, but the house is nearly paid off as it is. If I do choose to go the route of renting, I could still receive a steady income from it as long as the tenants aren't the kind that don't pay rent and destroy the house while they're in it.

My pink suitcase glares up at me from its spot on the floor, untouched from when I tossed it there five days ago. Glowering, I haul it onto the bed and decide to unpack and wash all the dirty clothes that are in it. Turning it over to dump it out, a sparkle catches my eye as I sort through the thick sweaters and fuzzy sock balls.

Nestled amongst my clothes is a letter. A letter with something attached to it. Something that looks startlingly familiar. Adrenaline pumps through me as I reach for it with shaky fingers. Tiffany's necklace is taped to a simple page of cream-colored paper with what I assume is Jonathan's handwriting scrawled across it.

EVELYN,

I'M SORRY FOR LEAVING WITHOUT SAYING GOODBYE. I DIDN'T WANT YOU TO WAKE UP ALONE, BUT I KNEW IF I STAYED, I'D ASK YOU TO STAY, TOO.

THIS WEEKEND MADE ME FEEL ALIVE AGAIN. YOU MADE ME FEEL ALIVE AGAIN. YOU MADE ME IMAGINE A WORLD THAT ISN'T SO DARK ALL THE TIME. THAT ISN'T A CONSTANT REMINDER OF EVERYTHING I'VE DONE WRONG, BUT OF WHAT I COULD DO RIGHT, MOVING FORWARD. YOU'VE BEEN A RAY OF SUNSHINE IN MY DARK AND DESOLATE life, and I honestly can't imagine my world without you in it.

I put the necklace I had made for Tiffany with this letter because I never had the chance to give it to her before she died. In some strange way, I think it was always meant to be yours. Because I want to believe in Christmas miracles again, and I truly think you are mine.

I know it sounds crazy, I'm aware it's only been two days, but I think fate brought us together. And I know you have big plans. I don't want you to put anything on hold for me, and I don't want you to miss out on your grand adventures. But if there's even the slightest part of you that feels the same, that feels like we were meant to meet and explore this connection we've made, then wait for me. We can go on your trip together.

I'll be back later tonight. Wait for me at my cabin, the door is unlocked. Make yourself at home.

And if I've imagined it all, and you don't feel the same, then I wish you all of the happiness in the world. And I

A drop of water hits the page as tears start to fall from my eyes.

My fingers raise to cover my mouth and my chest tightens as I process the emotional sucker punch I've just been dealt.

The letter must have been sitting on top of the stuff in my suitcase, but I was so distraught when I packed that I never saw it.

He asked me to wait for him.

He felt the same way.

And while I *had* waited, of my own volition, it hadn't been for long enough.

It feels like heartburn has settled into my esophagus and my feet start to move before my brain can catch up. I'm down the stairs in seconds, not bothering to change or even put on shoes instead of my slippers. I may not have an address, but I know how to get back to Lake Town.

To Jonathan.

To my happy ever after.

chapter nine

There's a red Suburban in the driveway when I pull up to Jonathan's cabin. His truck isn't there, but it doesn't stop me from running up and pounding on the door in my oversized cardigan and slippers.

"Jonathan! Jonathan, it's me! Evelyn!" My hands ball into fists as I keep hitting the door over and over again, shouting his name.

Finally, after what seems like forever, the door swings open and a man I don't recognize glares out at me. He looks disheveled, like he just rolled out of bed, and he's holding a hunting rifle. "What the hell do you think you're doing, miss? Do you know what time it is?"

No, I don't, and words don't form as I try to look past his shoulder to see inside. Finally, I manage, "I'm sorry, sir. I'm looking for Jonathan."

He never mentioned any other family, or renting out his place, so I'm confused when a puzzled look crosses the man's face and pulls his features taut. "I don't know who the hell *Jonathan* is."

Shaking my head, I motion to the cabin. "This is his house."

"No. This is *my* house. Has been for years. Maybe you're thinking of the cabin across the lake." He motions to the place I stayed last weekend.

Shaking my head at him, I grow frustrated and shout, "No! No, I was *just* here this weekend! This *is* Jonathan's house! *I* stayed at the cabin across the lake last weekend!"

His face melts into a look of concern as he sets his rifle down right inside the door and takes a step out toward me, hands raised as if trying not to spook a frightened animal. "Now, now. No need to get hysterical, miss. I can assure you I've owned this home for years. Besides the cabin across the lake, there aren't any others around for miles. Maybe you just got turned around."

"I didn't get turned around!" Backing away, frustrated tears start to fall as I cup my hands around my mouth and yell, "Jonathan!"

"What is going on out here?!" A woman's voice sounds from behind the man, and through my tears, I see another shape join him.

"She's looking for someone named Jonathan," he explains to her.

"Honey, there's no Jonathan here. Just Martin, the kids, and me. And you're gonna frighten our little ones with all your shouting," she gently scolds.

Without another word, I turn and run back to my car, wiping at my face and shoving my messy bun that is threatening to fall out back to its rightful place on the top of my head. Whoever that couple is, they've got it wrong.

The decision to head to town is easy. It's late, but I have to see if Cee's coffee shop is still open, or even the grocery store where Jonathan was on a first name basis with the butcher.

My mind is reeling and my lungs burn as my chest tightens so painfully that I think my ribs might crush them. Shallow breaths are all that I can manage most of the way there, but by the time I pull into the grocery store lot, I've managed to pull myself together.

Cee's shop across the road is closed, but the store is still open. It's probably too late for the butcher to be there, but I make my way to the back anyway, hands shoved deep in the pockets of my heavy down jacket.

Luck is on my side, it seems, as the lights are being turned off behind the meat counter just as I approach it. Racking my brain for his name, when it comes to me, I nearly shout it just as he disappears from view. "Tommy!"

Seconds later, the big, burly man pokes his head around the corner. "Sorry, miss. Just closed up. If it's easy though, I can get ya something already cut. But the machines are-"

"I'm not here for that. Do you know what happened to Jonathan?" Cutting him off, I stand on my tiptoes to try and see him over the raised counter.

"I'm sorry, there's no Jonathan that works here." He looks puzzled.

"No, he doesn't work here. He comes all the time. We were just here last weekend. You asked him if he wanted his usual?" It feels like there's a shark swimming in my stomach, chomping away at the lining as Tommy shakes his head slowly.

"I'm sorry, miss. I don't know who you're talking about. I remember all my regulars—it's a small town. But I don't recognize the name Jonathan, and I woulda remembered ya from last weekend." The way he says it isn't creepy, but as sympathetic as the look on his face, and it somehow makes me feel worse.

My shoulders sag as tears start forming behind my eyes again. He doesn't say anything else, so I turn and head back out to my car. Part of me wishing he'll call out and say something like, *"Oh! Yes, I do remember him!"*

But he doesn't.

♡ ♡ ♡ ♡

There could be guests at the cabin I stayed at, but I don't care—wishing desperately for any sort of feeling, for any sort of connection, to Jonathan.

Everything is dark as I pull into the driveway. There are no lights on. No tracks in the driveway. No evidence that anyone has been here at all.

As I walk up the steps to the front door, I pause abruptly as I notice there's no wood in the shed. There had been plenty when I left, enough that it would have lasted at least a month. So, for it to be all gone means someone would have had to remove it.

It's odd.

An uneasy feeling coats my insides like grease in a frying pan, as I knock gently on the door. When there's no answer, I reach down and twist the knob, relieved to find it unlocked. But what I find knocks the breath from my lungs.

Gone is the magic that seemed to bleed from the place just last weekend. It's dimmer. Even the wood seems duller. All the decorations are gone, and the fireplace is cleaned out. It no longer smells like Christmas, but like mothballs and the beginning stages of decay, as if the cabin hasn't been cleaned, or even exposed to fresh air in months.

Swiping my index finger along the top of the kitchen counter, I find that there's a thick layer of dust covering it.

"What the hell?"

The stairs creak and groan under my feet as I climb them, only to find the bed gone once I reach the top. There isn't even a clean spot on the floor where it occupied. Turning to head into the bathroom, I twist the faucet on so I can splash some water on my face. But as the water struggles to sputter out, I jump back in alarm as a stream of rusty, reddish-brown water finally starts to pour from it.

It's the same way in the kitchen when I try that faucet instead.

Pulling Jonathan's letter out of my pocket, I sink onto the couch in the living room and stare at it, wondering how any of this is possible.

The letter is real.

It's as tangible as the necklace that now hangs around my neck. Reaching up, I grab the pendant as I read his words again.

These are *real*.

So how can everything else be so absolutely *wrong*?

Clutching the letter to my chest, a tidal wave of

tears erupts as I let out a sob, curling onto my side in the fetal position and crying until I fall asleep.

♡ ♡ ♡ ♡

*M*orning beams its buttery shafts of sunlight through the large windows, rousing me from sleep. The musty smell is overpowering, making me want to gag as soon as I sit up. Rubbing the sleep from my eyes, I get up quickly and head out to my car, taking in big gulps of fresh air on the way.

My destination is already open by the time I park my car and head across the street, wrenching the door to Cee's open with such force, it startles the occupants inside. Elsie, Judy, and Esther are in their same spot as before, glancing at me warily with curious gazes.

"That was quite the entrance there. This place is as old as I am, dear. You gotta be a little more gentle with its old bones," Cee says gently as I rush to the counter.

"Cee! Please tell me where Jonathan is. Or that you remember him? That you remember *me*?" I frantically plea.

She steps back, startled by the volume of my voice, and clutches a hand to her chest as she stares at me like I just grew another head right in front of her. "What are you going on about? Are you the girl that woke the McGillin's last night?"

Well, news sure travels fast around here.

Slowly, I take a step back away from the counter. "You have no idea who I am, do you?"

"I know you're causing trouble, and we don't quite like that around here. Now, I *don't* know who you are, dear. And I don't know who this Jonathan is either. But I do know that if you need help, Rudy down at the police station would be more than happy to help you. *Do* you need help, dear?" She looks at me with the same sympathy as Tommy did last night, and it hits me like a ton of bricks.

Maybe I'm going crazy.

Did I just imagine the entire thing last weekend?

I've heard there are people who switch personalities and do things that they later don't remember. What if this was like that?

Was it *me* who wrote the letter?

Me who bought the necklace?

All eyes are on me as I back up and turn to leave, only pausing for a moment as Cee calls out behind me. "I hope you find whoever it is you're looking for."

As much as I hope the same, I'm beginning to think it's not going to happen.

Feeling defeated, I go home, where the next two weeks are spent combing over every site I can find that mentions anything about a Jonathan, a Tiffany, and a Jenny in the same article. I make multiple calls to every business where I think he could have worked, from Sutton to Denver. He said he worked in the city, but never said *which* city.

A stroke of luck lets me find the booking email for the cabin deep in my deleted email folder–only to find that the link for the listing is broken. Upon further digging, I also discover that the money was returned to my bank account.

No reversal pending, or chargeback. The entire purchase is just gone. As if it were never made in the first place.

After multiple calls to my bank, and them not being able to give me any information on a charge that never existed, I pull the address of the cabin from the email and paste it into the search bar. Again, though, I find myself at a dead end. The cabin has no owners and no information on previous owners. No details on previous sales or anything to suggest that it's currently for sale.

With that address, I *am* able to find information on the sale of the McGillin's cabin. But just as Martin had said, the cabin has belonged to them for years.

During those two weeks, the residents of Lake

Town are graced with my presence each weekend, and it's only when Martin McGillin threatens a restraining order on my ass, do I make the hard decision not to go back.

Jonathan isn't there.

If he ever had been in the first place.

Those two weeks turn into a month, and a month turns into two. Most everything that needs to be removed from my parents' house and put into storage has been, and I make the decision to sell it.

It's time to let go of the past and move forward. I'll never let go of the memories I have of them—those will always stay with me, wherever I end up.

Just as real as my memories of that magical Christmas weekend with Jonathan.

Now, my solo adventure awaits.

An array of experiences are mine for the taking.

And who knows? When I return, perhaps the McGillin's will no longer remember the crazy girl who was searching for her Christmas miracle.

chapter ten

Ten months later

Sutton's sharp winter wind and swirling flurries make me want to get right back on a plane and head back somewhere warm, where the air doesn't hurt my face.

Ten months of the glowing sun in Greece, goddess retreats in Bali, and mountain hikes in Tanzania has done my soul wonders. My hair is bright, my skin golden, and my heart is happy. In a way, I feel as though Jonathan *did* go with me on my trip. Because the necklace he gave me never came off from around my neck, not once. So, if anything, he was with me in my heart.

Now that I'm back, the urge to try and find him again has completely taken over. There is still money left over from the sale of the house, and I'm considering hiring a private investigator to see if they would have better luck than I did.

With my laptop tucked tight under my arm, I step into a small coffee shop so that I can look up investigators in the area while I enjoy my coffee. Coming back to Sutton isn't just about trying to find out if Jonathan exists, though. All my stuff is in storage, and I'm still not sure if I want to buy a small place here or continue my travels.

For now, I'm staying at a hotel down the street for Christmas. Even though I'm alone, I can spend Christmas Eve and Day in the little restaurant connected to the lobby and pretend like I'm not.

A gush of cold air brushes my back as someone else enters the shop while I wait in line. The hairs on the back of my neck stand on end and I lift my hand to warm it back up, shifting my weight to the other foot as the person in front of me makes their order.

Plain black coffee. Bleh.

When they step away, the pretty cashier smiles down at me as she asks what I'd like.

"I'll take a peppermint mocha breve, please."

"That's *your* drink, Daddy!" a small voice squeals behind me.

Turning, I look over my shoulder, offering a smile to the little girl standing there before looking up at her dad.

My heart stops as my eyes widen and his name leaves my lips in a surprised whisper. "Jonathan?"

He looks different. Leaner, freshly shaven, *happier*.

But it *is* him, and he tilts his head in surprise, opening his mouth to ask, "I'm sorry, do we know each other?"

Head reeling, I turn to face him fully. The little girl who is holding his hand tightly looks familiar, and I realize with startling clarity that it's Jenny.

How is that possible?

Absentmindedly, I reach up to finger the necklace that's resting at the hollow of my throat. His eyes track the movement and widen slightly when he sees the North Star pendant that he gave me.

The one he had made for his wife.

"I'm sorry, I don't know…this is weird," I finally manage breathily.

He's about to say something when a feminine, musical voice sounds behind him. "Jonathan, darling. Will you get a blueberry muffin as well?"

He turns to look over his shoulder, revealing Tiffany. She's sitting at a table along the wall–alive–and absolutely stunning with her glossy chocolate waves and bright blue eyes. "Sure thing, babe," he tells her.

What kind of alternate reality have I stepped into? Was I dreaming? This has to be a bad dream, right?

But it doesn't seem like a dream at all.

And how could it be bad if, however strange it may be, Tiffany and Jenny were here? Alive and well.

Jonathan looks so happy. So different than the man I met a year ago.

But you don't age backward.

And you can't come back from the dead.

Tears line my eyes as I quickly turn back to the coffee counter and say over my shoulder, "I'm sorry you just reminded me of someone I knew once."

"What a coincidence his name was also Jonathan," he replies smoothly. A hint of curiosity laces his tone, and I know I need to get out of there before I make a fool of myself. "If you don't mind me asking, where did you get that necklace?"

My eyes close, the tears threatening to fall as I attempt to get a hold of my emotions. It takes a few seconds before I answer without looking back at him. "From someone very dear to me."

"It's just strange because it looks exactly like the one I designed for my wife. The jeweler said they wouldn't repeat the design–"

"It was given to me a long time ago," I cut him off.

Or a long time in the future?

I have no clue *what* is *what* anymore, and I don't like the feeling that's swirling in my chest. But I'm relieved to know it wasn't a dream.

He's real.

He's here.

But he can never be mine.

Jonathan makes the humming noise I'd gotten

used to last Christmas, and it's so nostalgic that I nearly turn to embrace him, even though I know it'll make me look like a lunatic.

Paying the cashier, who has been patiently waiting for our little exchange to end, as she gives me a concerned look I slip a five-dollar bill in the tip jar before moving to the other end of the counter where my drink will come out.

I'm aware that Jonathan's eyes continue to dart over to me, trying to figure out who I am and how I knew his name. Why I'm wearing his wife's necklace.

Doing my best to keep my eyes focused on the barista making drinks, eventually my eyes dart over to him and our gazes lock. And I can't look away.

I knew if I stayed, I'd ask you to stay, too.

The words from his letter rush back to me. At this point, I've memorized the entire thing, but the note is tucked away in my wallet at all times. The paper creased and words smudged in some places where my errant tears have fallen. But even after all this time, I keep it with me–always.

Jenny looks like she's trying to get his attention, but it's focused solely on me. And just as it looks as though he's going to come over and say something more, I realize that I can't handle talking to him again. Tearing my eyes away from his, I turn and walk down the hallway to the bathroom. Tears fall freely down my face as I hastily wipe at them, pushing the door open and moving to brace my arms on the countertop.

The only way I kept convincing myself it was all real was the letter and the necklace. Those, and the memory of his touch. Of his gentle kisses and the way he held me as we slept.

Abruptly, the door to the bathroom swings open, causing me to jump. It's Tiffany, and she gives me a warm smile as our eyes connect in the mirror.

"Sorry, I didn't mean to scare you," she says in her musical tone.

Shaking my head, I offer a smile back. "It's okay. I'm just jumpy today."

Because I know what it feels like to sleep next to your husband in the future.

In the future.

I'm losing my damn mind.

Tiffany goes into the last stall, and I pretend like I'm washing my hands after wiping the remnants of my tears away. When she comes back out, I'm still staring at my face in the mirror, trying to make any sort of sense out of this situation.

Before I even know what I'm saying, I hear the words leave my mouth, "Your daughter is adorable."

Smiling as she washes her hands, she replies, "Thank you. She's a handful. We're about to embark on a six-hour road trip to go see her grandparents for Christmas. My husband has to stay in town for work, so she wanted to meet him for a hot chocolate before we get on the road. Like a six-year-old needs sugar before that long of a drive, right?"

Grabbing a paper towel, she turns and smiles as my brain is busy doing cartwheels in my head. I feel like that meme with the blonde lady and the mathematical equations as I work out what Tiffany just said.

Jonathan told me that his wife and daughter died in a car accident at Christmas. He said that he had to work and couldn't go with them. This *had* to be that moment.

For reasons I don't know, can't even begin to comprehend, fate has put me here today. In *this* coffee shop at *this* specific moment.

Images of that weekend a year ago flood my memory as I realize that I can try and stop the accident from happening again.

Tiffany is already reaching for the door when I spin and shout, "Don't go!"

My voice reverberates in the small space, and she jumps, turning to face me. "I'm sorry?"

"Don't go," I repeat.

The silence stretches between us as she looks at me curiously. Fumbling for something to say, I shrug my shoulder slightly. "No one should be alone at Christmas. If your husband can't go with you, you should stay."

Tiffany shakes her head slightly but still remains quiet, confusion spread across her beautiful face. My hands intertwine as I start to nervously pick at my nails. "I'm sorry. I don't mean to sound like I'm judging you for leaving. I'm not, I swear. I just…I lost my parents at Christmas a few years ago. I'm usually alone at this time of the year, and it's my favorite holiday, so it sucks. You know? I'm sure it would mean a lot to him if you stayed."

Her confused look is replaced by one of empathy, then contemplation. "It's his, too. My husband's that is. It's just been a tradition to go North every year. I never even considered staying."

"I'm sure he'll appreciate it, even if he says it's okay to go." Because he *did* tell her it was okay. Because he didn't want her to miss out on Christmas with her mom and dad. He would have never told her he wanted her to stay.

Tiffany smiles sadly at me. "I'm sorry about your parents."

Shaking my head, I briefly wonder if somehow they're alive again. But deep down, I know that whatever magic happened up at the cabin, stayed at the cabin. "Thank you."

Awkwardly, I turn and walk into one of the stalls, locking myself inside without another word. A few moments later, I hear her leave and I let out a long, shuddered breath. Spending the next few minutes trying to regain my composure, I quickly exit the bathroom and hastily walk down the hall to grab my drink that's sitting at the end of the pick-up counter.

My eyes remain on the door as I try to leave without looking over at Jonathan and his family. But an awareness creeps down my spine as if someone is watching me, and my eyes stray to their table. Jenny is sipping her hot chocolate happily while Jonathan and Tiffany are sitting against the wall–their eyes on me.

Jonathan gives me a slight nod and a tight smile, his curious gaze still present on his face. Tiffany beams at me as if we're old friends. She nods her head as well, an unspoken *thank you* hanging in the air between us. A smile stretches across my face as I realize that she might take my advice and decide to stay.

With a small wave at them, I push open the door and step out into the flurries that are still swirling in the harsh wind.

Merry Christmas, Jonathan.

"Alright, Bagel. Where to next, buddy?" Reaching over, I scratch my new beagle pup behind the ears as he finishes his cup of whipped cream in the passenger seat.

Two days ago, on my way into a mall because I had a craving for a Hot Dog On A Stick, I happened to glance into the window of a pet store.

When I saw him staring at me with his big brown eyes, and ears that seemed too big for his head, I knew right away that I had to have him. It didn't matter that I didn't exactly have a place to live, the hotel was pet friendly. And though the little dude was already estimated to be a year old, the pet handler in the shop said he didn't respond to any sort of name. But the moment I called him Bagel, his ears perked up and he let out a short yip while wagging his tail.

It's been a week since that day in the coffee shop. A week since I realized that my time at the cabin a year ago was a magical, mystical phenomenon. Currently, I'm parked on the side of the street, sucking on a candy cane with a clear view of the coffee shop, as I watch Jonathan, Tiffany, and Jenny walk inside.

I'm not a stalker, I swear.

Words can't describe how incredibly pleased I am that Tiffany heeded my advice and hadn't gone on the road trip. I've come back to the shop every day this week to see if they'd come back.

Now that I know they are safe, and that Jonathan hasn't lost his family, I feel a sense of accomplishment and also one of completeness. Over the last week, I've come to terms with what happened. In some paranormal way, I feel like I was sent to Sutton Lake last year for a reason. Jonathan and I *needed* each other then. And in some twisted Christmas miracle type of way, fate had answered and delivered us to each other.

I don't dwell on what would have happened had I found the note before I went home. If I had, I would have marched across the lake and never left Jonathan's embrace again. My heart was broken after I found his letter and went back to find that nothing that weekend was as it seemed.

Jonathan and I hadn't spent enough time together to fall in love, but we'd found our way back to each other, anyway. And I am convinced now, more than ever, that people come into your life for a reason–whether it's for a little while or they end up being your happily ever after.

Everything–every *person*–has a purpose.

Jonathan is happy. *I'm* happy.

Bagel is my companion now, and we need to decide where we're gonna spend New Years.

My cousin Kendall's name pops up on my dashboard screen, and I tear my eyes away from the happy family to press accept. "Hi, babe."

"Evie! It's so good to hear your voice! How was your trip?" Her cheerful voice rings out through my speakers.

"It was absolutely amazing. I'll have to tell you all about it next time I see you. It's so much to say over the phone. And the photos! Oh my God, Kendall, you'll die."

Bagel finishes his whipped cream and lays down, licking his maw before settling down in his bed. Maybe we'll go somewhere warm, so he can run in the sand and stretch out in the sun.

"Well, what are you doing for New Years? You could come this way and stay with us for a little while?" she asks slyly.

She sounds like she's scheming, causing me to laugh as I tell her, "I don't have any plans. But I do have a dog now."

"Excellent! We have a yard. And Bree's kids love dogs, so as long as it's good with kids, it should be fine!"

Chicago for New Year's, hmm? That doesn't sound terrible, I guess.

"Sure, that sounds great! It's gonna take like a whole day to get there, though."

"Just keep me updated on your progress! Love you. Excited to see you!"

"Love you too. See you soon."

A knock on the window makes me jump and let out a squeak as Bagel lets out a startled bark. Grabbing my chest as if it will help calm my racing heart, I push the button to roll down the window as I turn my head.

Only to come face to face with Jonathan himself.

Bagel bounds across my lap, tail wagging as he greets him, and Jonathan's face lights up as he reaches out to scratch his ears. "Hey there, buddy. What's your name?"

It takes a moment for words to find me as I watch him fawn over the dog he's always wanted with the name he's always wanted to give it. My voice is quiet as I tell him, "It's Bagel."

Jonathan's eyes snap to mine, his smile faltering as his brows scrunch together. "No way, really? That's crazy, I've always wanted a beagle named Bagel."

I know.

The words almost leave my mouth but remain unspoken. "Was there something I can help you with?"

His cheeks redden, and he looks embarrassed. Memories of him flushed and breathing heavily underneath me flash through my mind before he answers me. "I, uh, I noticed you when I was walking into the coffee shop. This is gonna sound weird but, I've been thinking of you all week. I can't explain it. I just feel like I know you somehow. Do you live around here?"

Blushing, I look down at Bagel, who is now

settled on my lap with his head perched on the window frame as Jonathan continues to rub his head. "Not anymore."

"I don't mean to sound like a creep. I hope I'm not making you uncomfortable. It's just…you're familiar. And I get this sense…like you are a very important person to my family."

His eyes are drilling a hole into the side of my face and I glace up at him, lips pulling into a tight smile as my heart clenches. "Perhaps we knew each other in another life."

My eyes stray to the bag in his free hand, and his gaze follows mine. His cheeks redden further as he shoves the bag through the window and into my face. "Please don't think I'm creepy. But I got you this. It's a shit thank you, but Tiffany told me what you said to her in the bathroom last week. Because of you, she decided to stay in town for Christmas, and there was a bad accident that her and our daughter could have been involved in. So, I'm really thankful to you."

The words leave him in a flustered rush as I gingerly take the bag from him. Bagel immediately pokes his nose inside as I open it to reveal a large blueberry muffin.

Even now, still trying to feed me.

My cheeks warm as I remember his words to me a year ago, right before I went down on him. Shaking my head slightly, I roll the bag up and maneuver Bagel back to the passenger seat.

"Thank you. That was kind of you."

"Would you…would you maybe want…to join us?" he asks as he nervously scratches the back of his neck.

My mind is made up before he finishes asking, knowing where his words are heading. With a slight shake of my head and an apologetic smile, I tell him, "That's really nice of you to ask. But I actually need to get on the road. I'm happy for you, Jonathan. I'm really happy your wife stayed."

The words are genuine and we share a smile as he nods slightly, looking a little lost–as if he wants to continue speaking but isn't sure what to say. Turning on my car, I buckle Bagel in and then secure my seatbelt before turning to give him a small wave.

"Goodbye, Jonathan."

"Goodbye–what is your name?"

His question is muffled by my window rolling up. Flashing him a genuine smile, I shake my head and give him a small wave before pulling away from the curb.

Giving him my name won't do either of us any good. All that matters is that everything is the way it should be.

The way it was always meant to be.

epilogue

*B*agel and I pull over to spend the night in a seedy hotel just off the highway, so it's mid-afternoon by the time we get into Chicago. Kendall, bless her heart, rushes me into the bathroom as soon as I get there for reasons that I cannot comprehend. Showering wasn't on my mind this morning when I left the hotel, mainly because the bathroom looked like it was growing a science project in it, but I knew I didn't stink.

"People are coming over soon! You want to look your best, don't you? Don't worry about this cutie pie, I'll look after him," she coos as she sticks her face in Bagel's and nuzzles his nose, letting him give her sloppy kisses.

"Hey! Gettin' a little too fresh with my woman there, mutt!" Mark hollers from his place on the couch.

Giggling, I take my stuff into the guest room and shower, taking the time to curl my hair and even put on a little makeup. Kendall's friends—Bree, Charleigh, and Daphne—are the nicest group of females you'll ever meet, but Jesus, they are too hot for their own damn good.

Once I'm convinced I won't feel like an absolute troll for the evening, I put on a cute pair of jeans, tuck in an oversized cashmere sweater, and pull on a pair of low-heeled, knee-high boots to complete my outfit. Kendall said they were going to start a fire in the pit in the backyard and let the kids run around with sparklers.

"Will there be any fireworks? I'm slightly worried about that with Bagel—I haven't had him long enough to know if it will bother him or not," I ask once I've joined her in the kitchen.

"You look so cute! To answer your question, no. Our neighborhood is a no fireworks zone, which I'm thankful for. We'll probably hear them and maybe even see them, but they shouldn't be too loud. And Eric is bringing Archer, so Bagel will have someone to play with."

As soon as the words leave her mouth, a giant German shepherd bounds into the kitchen, seeking Bagel out like a bloodhound would a deer. He whines sharply, tail wagging as he attempts to stick his nose in Bagel's butt.

"OUTSIDE!" Kendall shouts, moving to open the door to the backyard.

"Archer! Sorry, Kendall. I'll clean up the snow," a comforting voice says behind me.

Archer races out the door and Bagel struggles in my arms, trying to follow him, so I let him go and watch as they start to chase each other and play in the snow. A figure comes up beside me and I look over to see a tall, dark-haired man laughing quietly as he watches them, a peppermint stick hanging from his mouth.

He turns his blue eyes to mine and holds out a hand, pulling out the candy before flashing me a mouth full of pearly whites. "Eric Adams. You must be Evie? Kendall tells me you've just returned from abroad! I'm jealous."

If I'm remembering my facts correctly, this is Kendall's friend Daphne's husband, so I try to quell the butterflies in my stomach that flutter as I shake his hand. "Interested in traveling?"

Before he can answer, Daphne steps into the kitchen behind us, breathing heavily as she lays a hand on her gigantic stomach. "I can't wait to get this thing out of me. It's sucking all of my life force and I can't even have a drink to fill my mental bank."

She smiles when she sees me and reaches out for a hug. "Evie! It's been too long! How are you? How was your trip?"

After we embrace, I return her smile and nod to her belly. "It was good. I know, it's been forever. Congratulations to you guys!"

Looking between her and Eric, I'm confused when they look at each other in confusion and then burst into laughter. "No, no, no! We got divorced a few years ago. I'm remarried now. He'll be here a little later. He's currently dealing with a work crisis. And I am about to have a crisis if I don't eat something!"

My stomach decides that's a good time to let out a loud gurgle, causing Kendall and Eric to both laugh as my cheeks grow warm. "I could eat, too," I say sheepishly.

"Well, that's good, because I cooked *a lot*!" Kendall exclaims, unwrapping a stack of paper plates. "Dish up!"

After Eric makes Daphne a plate, and makes sure she's comfortable in Mark's recliner—plate perched on her belly—he takes a seat beside me at the kitchen table.

"For being divorced you sure are sweet on her still." The words leave my mouth before I can stop them and I avoid the sharp turn of his head, staring down at my plate instead.

He lets out a soft laugh and leans over to say quietly, "Daph and I will always be friends. We went through a lot together, and I'm not the kind of person to just drop someone after a difficult breakup. Besides, we mutually decided to split. There's no hard feelings there."

"That's admirable of you. Are you remarried as well?" Picking at the yam casserole, I can't help but compare them to Jonathan's.

Kendall's aren't as good.

"Nah, I haven't met anyone that understands the dynamic this group has. I was even a groomsman for Henry at their wedding. Not many women are comfortable with how close we all are." He takes a large bite of his burger and turns to me again. "So tell me about your trip!"

The interest he's showing in me has me puzzled, but I whip my phone out and start to flip through my photos, spending the next hour telling him tales of my adventures. Eventually, Daphne's husband shows up looking like a tall drink of Superman-flavored water.

Eric laughs at my wide eyes after Henry walks outside and leans down to whisper, "He gets that reaction a lot."

Bree and her husband, Will, also show up with their three kids. And we all move outside so the kids can play with sparklers as the dogs chase them around. To my relief, Bagel is doing well with the children, and the distant sound of the fireworks as they go off throughout the night.

Eventually, Bree puts the kids to bed, and Archer and Bagel curl up with them on the oversized couch in the living room.

When Eric disappears into the house to grab us both another drink, he tells me he'll check on the dogs. As he leaves, Kendall sidles up to me and nudges my shoulder.

"You and Eric seem to be getting along pretty well." The way she says it hits me suddenly, and her lips pull up into a grin as she waggles her eyebrows.

"You're trying to set us up, aren't you?"

"What? Me? Yes. Yes, I am." She sips her wine and shrugs. "You two have a lot in common. I think you'd be so cute together."

"And what if I was dating someone already?" Unbelievable. But honestly, no, it's very believable.

My cousin is a self-proclaimed matchmaker. This would be her bread and butter if she wasn't so good at the job she already has, I swear.

"If you were, you would have said so when I asked you to come stay with us. But no, you said '*I have a dog.*'"

"Fair," I deadpan.

"Mmmhmm," she singsongs as she walks away just as Eric makes it back to my side.

"So, where were we? Ah, yes. The Pacific Northwest. Great hiking there! Easier to take a dog there than to Europe. Unless you planned on bringing Bagel to the Dolomites?"

He hands me a beer and a peppermint stick, already sucking on his own, and I can't help but look at him in a different light now. Part of me wonders if he's in on it, but his actions all night have seemed genuine. He's all smiles with a happy-go-lucky demeanor. His Hershey's bar hair falls into his eyes as he speaks, and he's got stubble on his face as though he hasn't shaved for a few days.

He's attractive.

But I'm not sure I'm ready for romance. At least not something super serious.

"I never thought of it, honestly. I didn't plan on traveling internationally with him, unless it was to Mexico or Canada, where I can drive."

"Champagne time everyone!" A voice rings out and I look over to see Charleigh come through the doors holding two bottles of champagne. There's another woman I don't know following her with more bottles, and two men I don't recognize who are attempting to hold a bunch of champagne flutes.

Eric leans down so that I can hear him over all the commotion. "Have you ever thought about hiking the Oregon coast? I was thinking of doing it this Easter with Archer. Maybe you and Bagel could come along?"

My eyes snap to his as I ask, "Did you know Kendall is trying to set us up?"

He has the grace to look embarrassed and dips his head, cheeks growing red. "Truthfully? She didn't come right out and say that. But she *did* mention that we might enjoy each other's company because we have a lot of things in common."

I'm silent as Charleigh comes over and gives us both a glass before she pulls me in for a hug. "You look great, Evie! We've missed you around here! Tell me you're staying a little while?"

Shrugging, I tell her quietly, "I'm not sure, yet." My eyes flit back to Eric's, who is now watching me like a puppy who got caught chewing up the couch.

"Well, you should! We'd be happy to have you." She continues on her journey of passing out champagne flutes.

Eric doesn't say anything when she leaves, and I'm left with a feeling in my stomach that I can't quite place. "I'm not sure I'm ready for something romantic."

Shouts raise up as the majority of the backyard starts the countdown to midnight, everyone pairing off with their partners, leaving me and Eric to share an awkward smile.

"Ten, nine..."

He takes a sip of his champagne and shakes his

head. "That's more than okay, Evie. I'm okay with just being friends."

"*Eight, seven…*"

"No, I mean, I'm not ready right *now*. That's not to say I won't be, sometime, in the future." Why the fuck do I have to be so awkward?

"Evie–"

"*Six, five, four…*"

"And I should be, really. I mean, it's not like I just got out of a relationship. If anything, I just came back from being in a relationship with myself for the better part of the last year. But this whole thing happened last Christmas that was really weird–"

"Evie–"

"*Three, two…*"

"And I kind of thought this guy was supposed to be like my soulmate or something–"

"*ONE! HAPPY NEW YEAR!*" Multiple people yell from all around us.

"Evie!" Eric shouts over all the noise, and I shut my mouth and stop blurting out words.

He takes a few steps toward me, leaning down to set his drinks on the ground before he straightens and grabs my hand. As everyone around us leans in to kiss their partners, Eric lifts my hand to his lips and lays a gentle kiss on the back of it. My cheeks warm as I watch him, his eyes never leaving mine as he grins against my hand.

"I'm a patient man, Evie. And I know a good thing when I see one. There's nothing wrong with just being friends for now, if that's what you want. But you gotta admit, it's always nicer to have someone on the trails with you. And no one should hike alone during the holidays."

His smooth words cause those little peppermint butterflies to return, brushing my insides with their tingly wings as he looks at me expectantly. Jonathan flashes through my mind, and I reach up to grab the pendant at my neck. I may have missed my chance at a life with him, but I won't miss another opportunity if I can help it. Eric seems like a great guy; all I have to do is take the leap.

Stepping outside of my comfort zone, I press up on my tiptoes and wrap my arms around Eric's neck, pulling him closer. A surprised smile tugs at his lips, and just before I close the distance between us, I say, "You're right. No one should be alone for the holidays."

Wish you
were here!

-Evie & Eric

INTERESTED IN DAPHNE AND HENRY'S STORY?

CHECK OUT MY DEBUT NOVEL WHERE THE FLOWERS BLOOM

AVAILABLE ON KINDLE UNLIMITED AND WHEREVER BOOKS ARE SOLD

afterword

I always knew from the start that I wanted Evie's journey to go the way it did. From the very first spark, I knew she and Jonathan wouldn't end up together but needed their weekend to move on with life.

There was a lot of discussion with my alphas and betas about what exactly happened at the cabin and why it wasn't explained. But that's the thing…there is no explanation. It's a Christmas miracle that can't be explained, just like the movie The Lakehouse, which heavily inspired this book.

Bringing the Where the Flowers Bloom crew back into the mix came to me about halfway through when I wasn't sure how the story would end beyond Evie and Jonathan running into each other. Eric kind of came out of nowhere and was like, "Remember when you told me I could have a happy ending too?"

And I was like, "I'm so sorry, my man, I totally forgot about you."

This story birthed another idea that may or may not come to fruition in the future. All I know is that I enjoy bringing my first-ever book babies back into the world.

And this certainly won't be the last time you see them ;)

acknowledgments

Thank you a million times over to Alex and Jessica, the best friends, book besties, and critique partners a girl could ask for.

Thank you to my betas, Ashley, Cady, Domenica, Kendra, and Kimberly, for wanting to read Christmas in June.

To my editor, Virginia, for always wanting to work, even when you're supposed to be recovering from surgery.

To my PA, Cassie, for always making life easier and for just being an amazing human being in general.

Thank you to Rachel McEwan for my beautiful cover and having the patience to deal with my crazy.

Last but never least, to all the readers who continue to take chances on indie authors. Thank you. We would be nothing without you.

about the author

D.L. Darby lives in Anchorage, Alaska, with her cat, dog, and husband.

When she's not working, reading, or writing, she's glued to the TV watching Miraculous Ladybug and Cat Noir—or watching Sex and the City for the millionth time.

also by d.l. darby

Where the Flowers Bloom

Slice of Temptation

Sweet as Sin